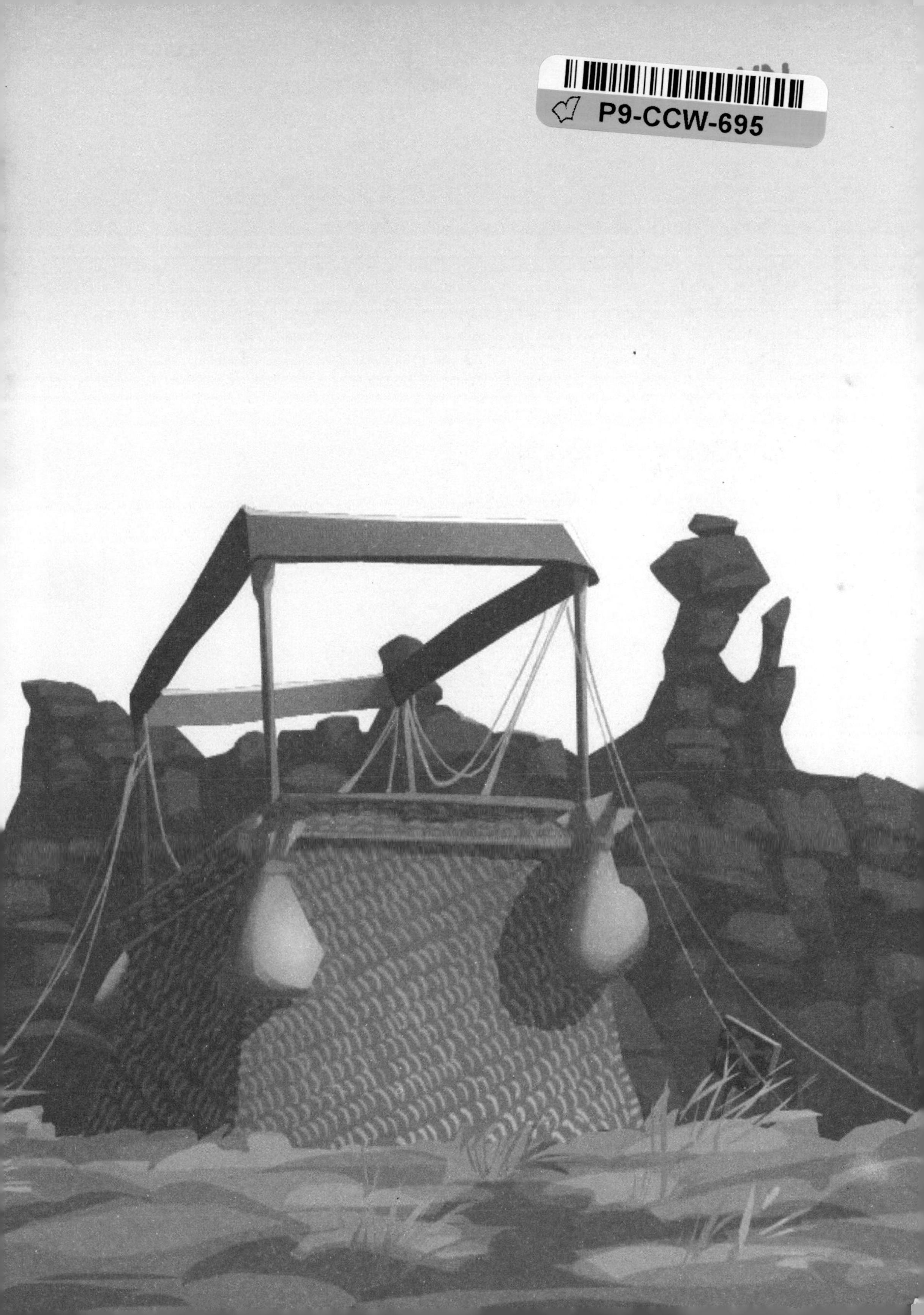

Geronimo Stilton ™ Reporter

PAPERCUTZ ™

Geronimo Stilton

GRAPHIC NOVELS AVAILABLE FROM PAPERCUTZ™

...ALSO AVAILABLE WHEREVER E-BOOKS ARE SOLD!

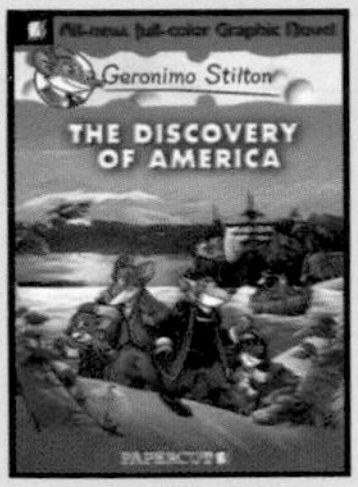

All-new, full-color Graphic Novel
Geronimo Stilton
THE DISCOVERY OF AMERICA

#1
"The Discovery of America"

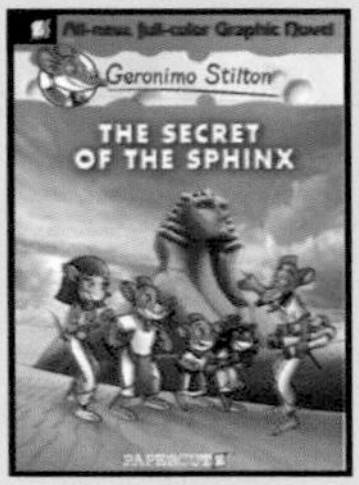

All-new, full-color Graphic Novel
Geronimo Stilton
THE SECRET OF THE SPHINX

#2
"The Secret of the Sphinx"

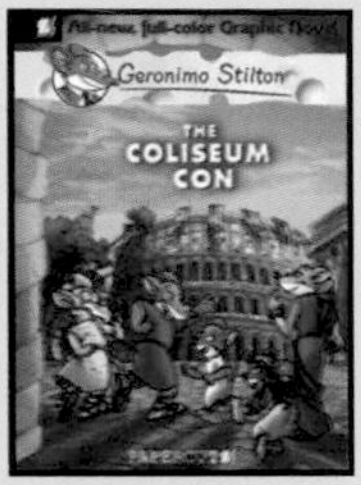

All-new, full-color Graphic Novel
Geronimo Stilton
THE COLISEUM CON

#3
"The Coliseum Con"

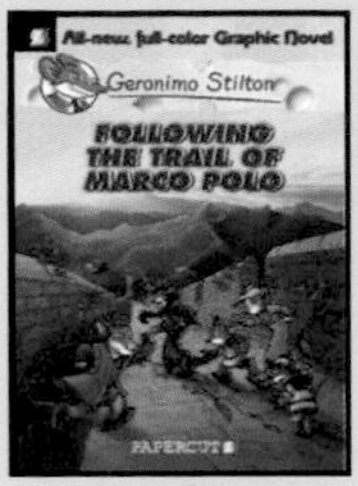

All-new, full-color Graphic Novel
Geronimo Stilton
FOLLOWING THE TRAIL OF MARCO POLO

#4
"Following the Trail of Marco Polo"

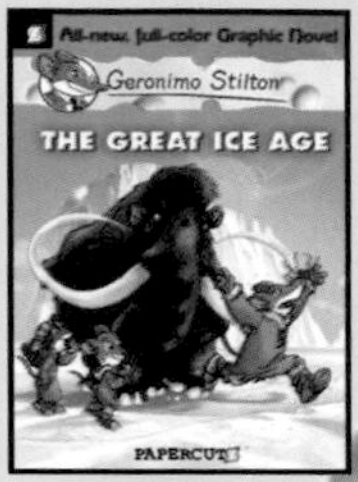

All-new, full-color Graphic Novel
Geronimo Stilton
THE GREAT ICE AGE

#5
"The Great Ice Age"

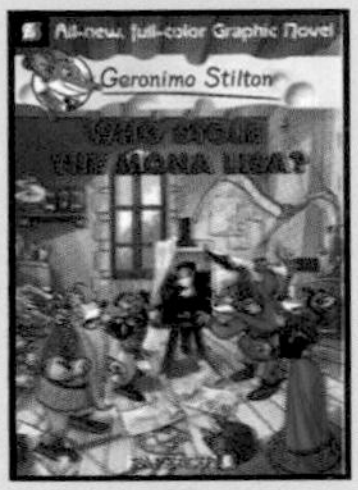

All-new, full-color Graphic Novel
Geronimo Stilton

#6
"Who Stole the Mona Lisa?"

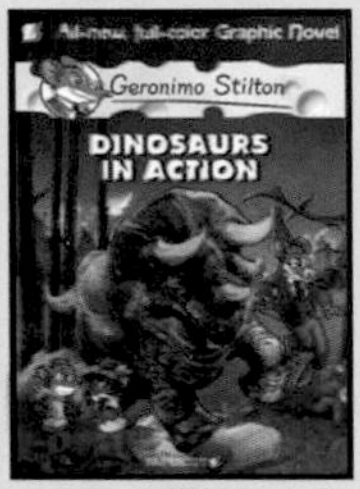

All-new, full-color Graphic Novel
Geronimo Stilton
DINOSAURS IN ACTION

#7
"Dinosaurs in Action"

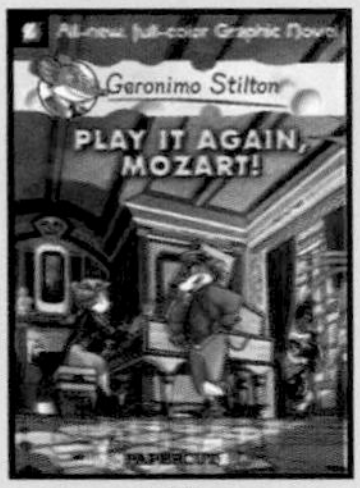

All-new, full-color Graphic Novel
Geronimo Stilton
PLAY IT AGAIN, MOZART!

#8
"Play It Again, Mozart!"

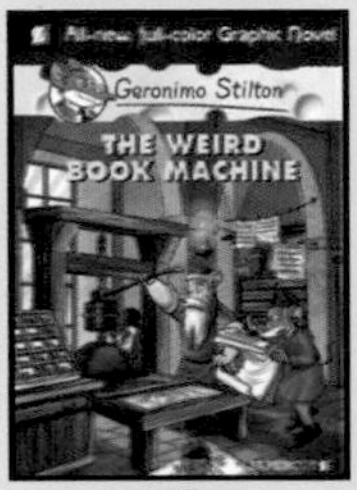

All-new, full-color Graphic Novel
Geronimo Stilton
THE WEIRD BOOK MACHINE

#9
"The Weird Book Machine"

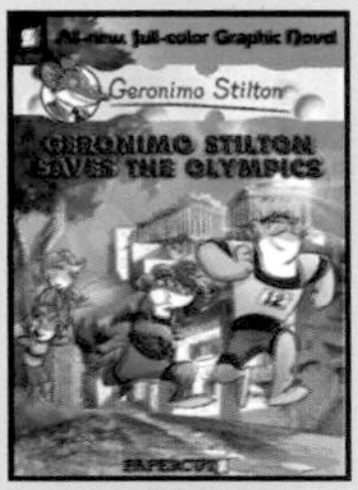

All-new, full-color Graphic Novel
Geronimo Stilton
GERONIMO STILTON SAVES THE OLYMPICS

#10
"Geronimo Stilton Saves the Olympics"

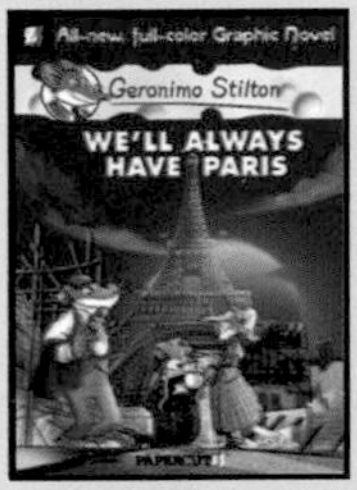

All-new, full-color Graphic Novel
Geronimo Stilton
WE'LL ALWAYS HAVE PARIS

#11
"We'll Always Have Paris"

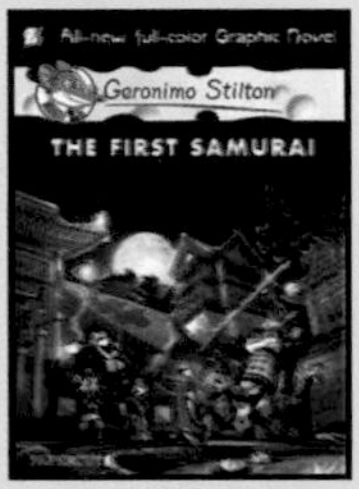

All-new, full-color Graphic Novel
Geronimo Stilton
THE FIRST SAMURAI

#12
"The First Samurai"

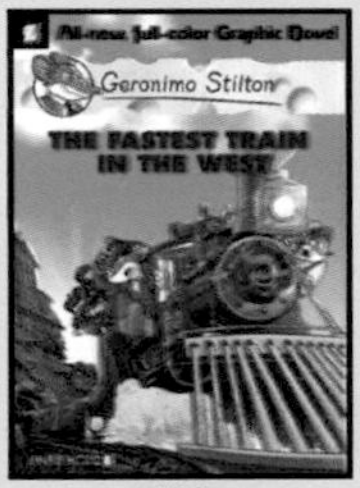

All-new, full-color Graphic Novel
Geronimo Stilton
THE FASTEST TRAIN IN THE WEST

#13
"The Fastest Train in the West"

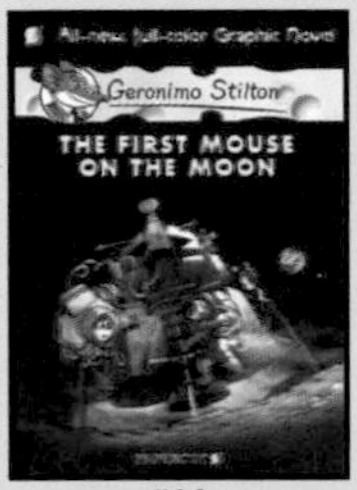

All-new, full-color Graphic Novel
Geronimo Stilton
THE FIRST MOUSE ON THE MOON

#14
"The First Mouse on the Moon"

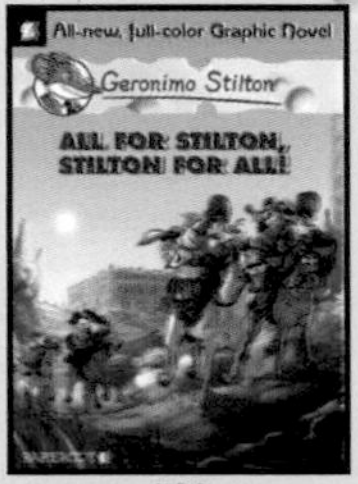

All-new, full-color Graphic Novel
Geronimo Stilton
ALL FOR STILTON, STILTON FOR ALL!

#15
"All for Stilton, Stilton for All!"

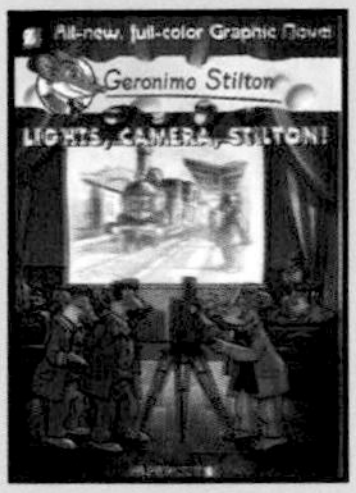

All-new, full-color Graphic Novel
Geronimo Stilton
LIGHTS, CAMERA, STILTON!

#16
"Lights, Camera, Stilton!"

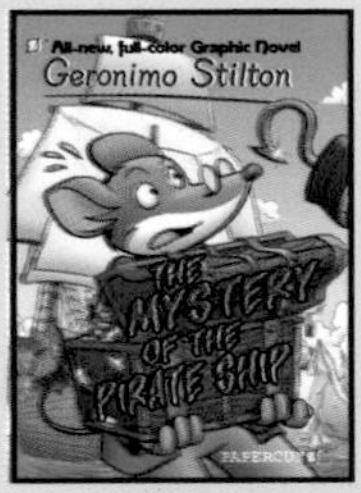

All-new, full-color Graphic Novel
Geronimo Stilton
THE MYSTERY OF THE PIRATE SHIP

#17
"The Mystery of the Pirate Ship"

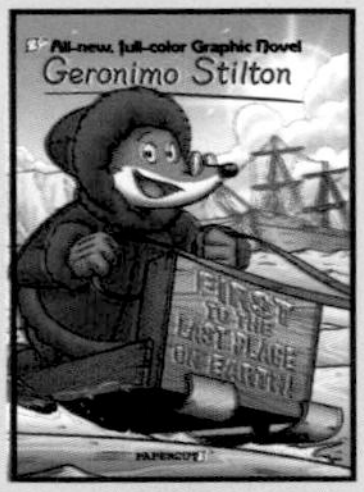

All-new, full-color Graphic Novel
Geronimo Stilton

#18
"First to the Last Place on Earth"

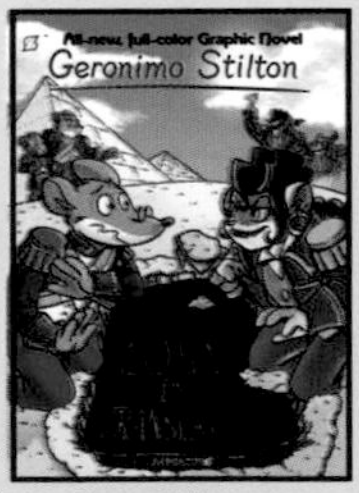

All-new, full-color Graphic Novel
Geronimo Stilton

#19
"Lost in Translation"

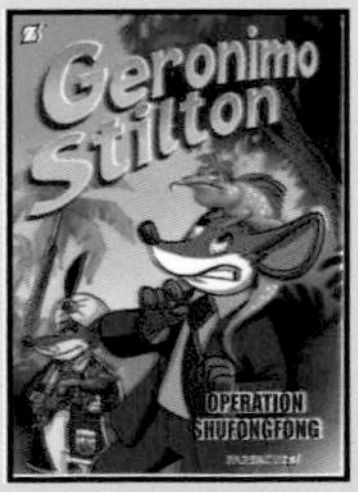

Geronimo Stilton
OPERATION SHUFONGFONG

#1
"Operation Shufongfong"

papercutz.com

GERONIMO STILTON graphic novels are available for $9.99 each only in hardcover. Available from booksellers everywhere. You can also order online from papercutz.com. Or call 1-800-886-1223, Monday through Friday, 9 – 5 EST. MC, Visa, and AmEx accepted. To order by mail, please add $5.00 for postage and handling for first book ordered, $1.00 for each additional book and make check payable to NBM Publishing.
Send to: Papercutz, 160 Broadway, Suite 700, East Wing, New York, NY 10038.

Geronimo Stilton™ Reporter

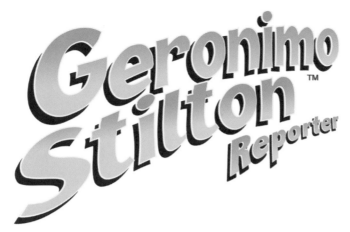

#3 STOP ACTING AROUND

By Geronimo Stilton

PAPERCUTZ™
NEW YORK

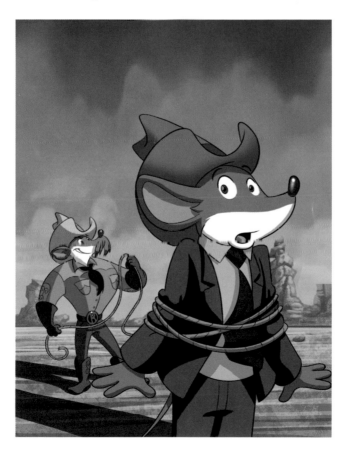

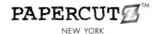

STOP ACTING AROUND

Text by Geronimo Stilton
Cover by ALESSANDRO MUSCILLO (artist) and CHRISTIAN ALIPRANDI (colorist)
Editorial supervision by ALESSANDRA BERELLO (Atlantyca S.p.A.)
Editing by LISA CAPIOTTO (Atlantyca S.p.A.)
Script by DARIO SICCHIO based on the episode by ROB HUMPHREY and JOHN BEHNKE
Art by ALESSANDRO MUSCILLO
Color by CHRISTIAN ALIPRANDI
Original Lettering by MARIA LETIZIA MIRABELLA

Based on an original idea by ELISABETTA DAMI.
Based on episode 3 of the Geronimo Stilton animated series, "*Ciak, si gira!*"

www.geronimostilton.com

JAYJAY JACKSON — Production
WILSON RAMOS JR. — Lettering
KARR ANTUNES — Editorial Intern
JEFF WHITMAN — Managing Editor
JIM SALICRUP
Editor-in-Chief

ISBN: 978-1-5458-0332-5

Printed in India
September 2019

Papercutz books may be purchased for business or promotional use.
For information on bulk purchases please contact
Macmillan Corporate and Premium Sales
Department at (800) 221-7945x5442.

Distributed by Macmillan
First Printing

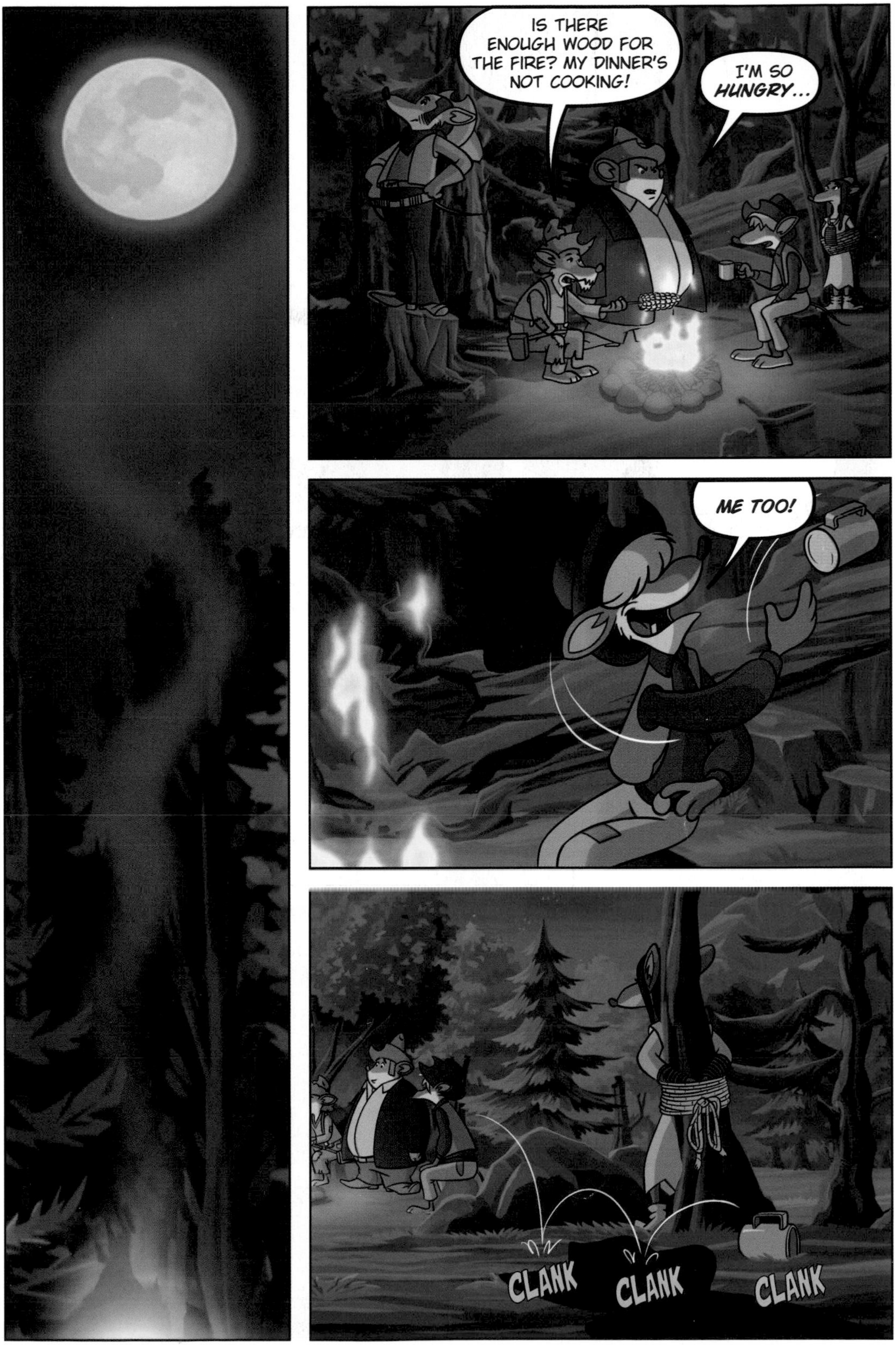
IS THERE ENOUGH WOOD FOR THE FIRE? MY DINNER'S NOT COOKING!
I'M SO *HUNGRY*...
ME TOO!
CLANK
CLANK
CLANK

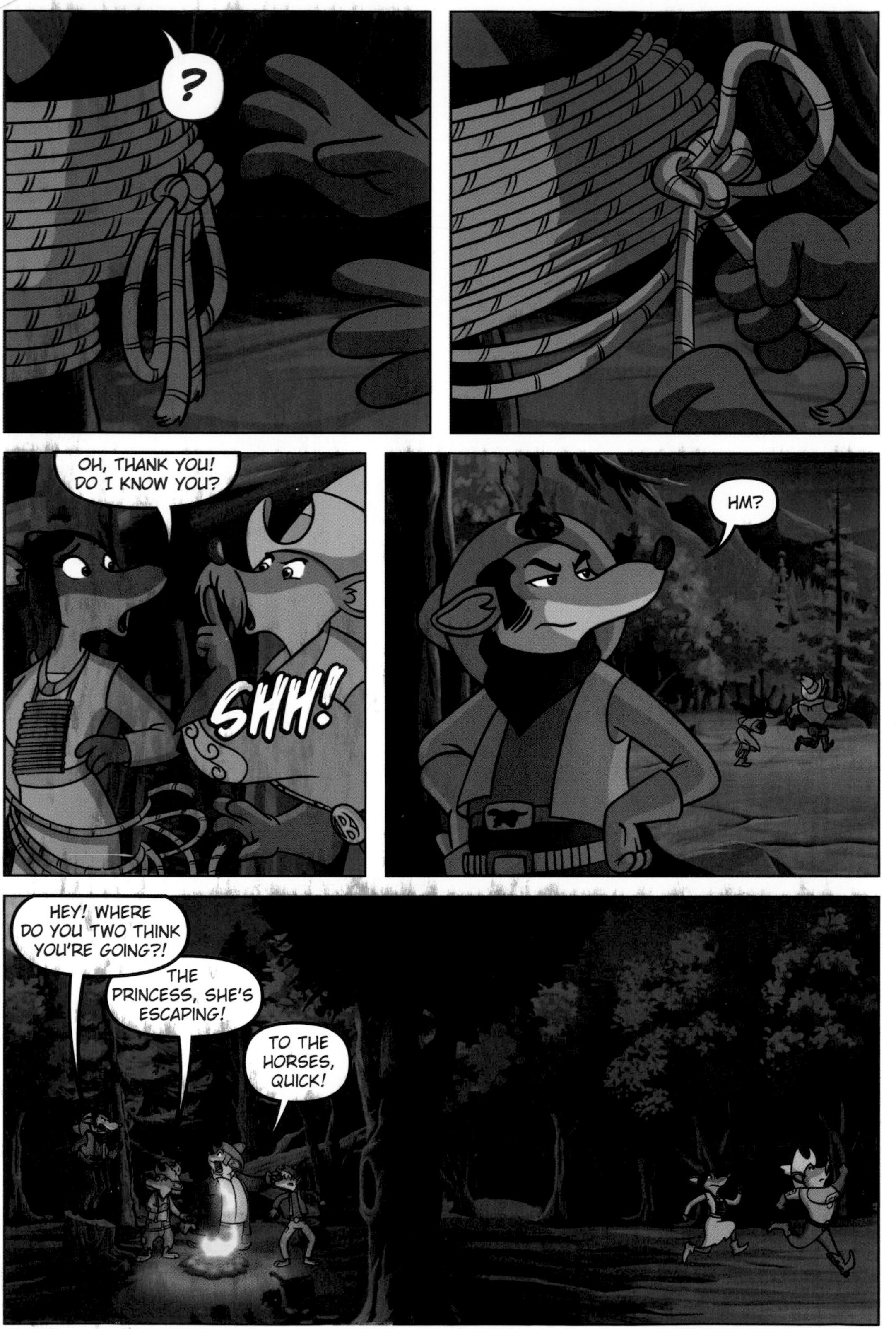
?
OH, THANK YOU! DO I KNOW YOU?
SHH!
HM?
HEY! WHERE DO YOU TWO THINK YOU'RE GOING?!
THE PRINCESS, SHE'S ESCAPING!
TO THE HORSES, QUICK!

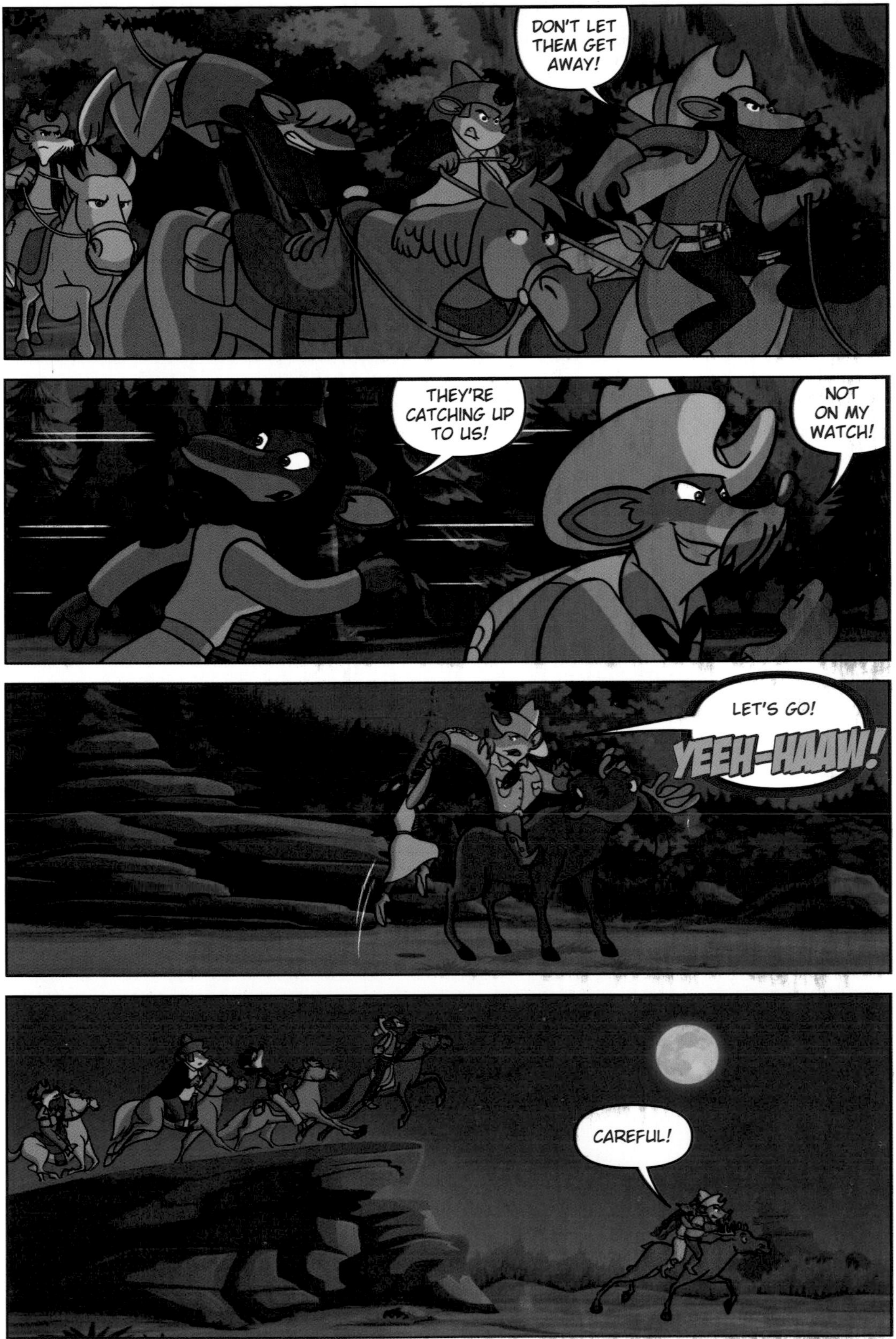
DON'T LET THEM GET AWAY!
THEY'RE CATCHING UP TO US!
NOT ON MY WATCH!
LET'S GO!
YEEH-HAAW!
CAREFUL!

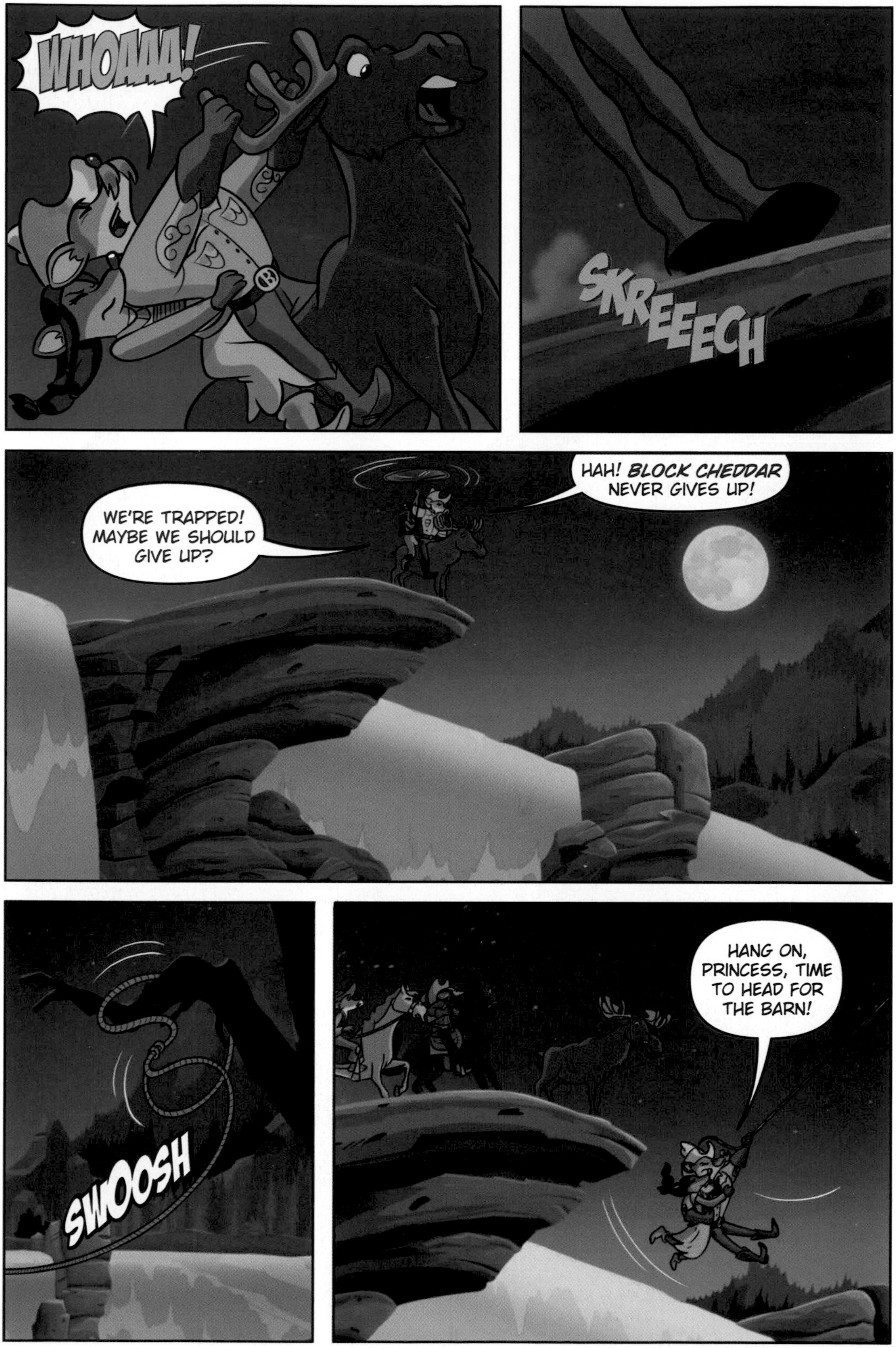
WHOAAA!
SKREEECH
WE'RE TRAPPED! MAYBE WE SHOULD GIVE UP?
HAH! BLOCK CHEDDAR NEVER GIVES UP!
SWOOSH
HANG ON, PRINCESS, TIME TO HEAD FOR THE BARN!

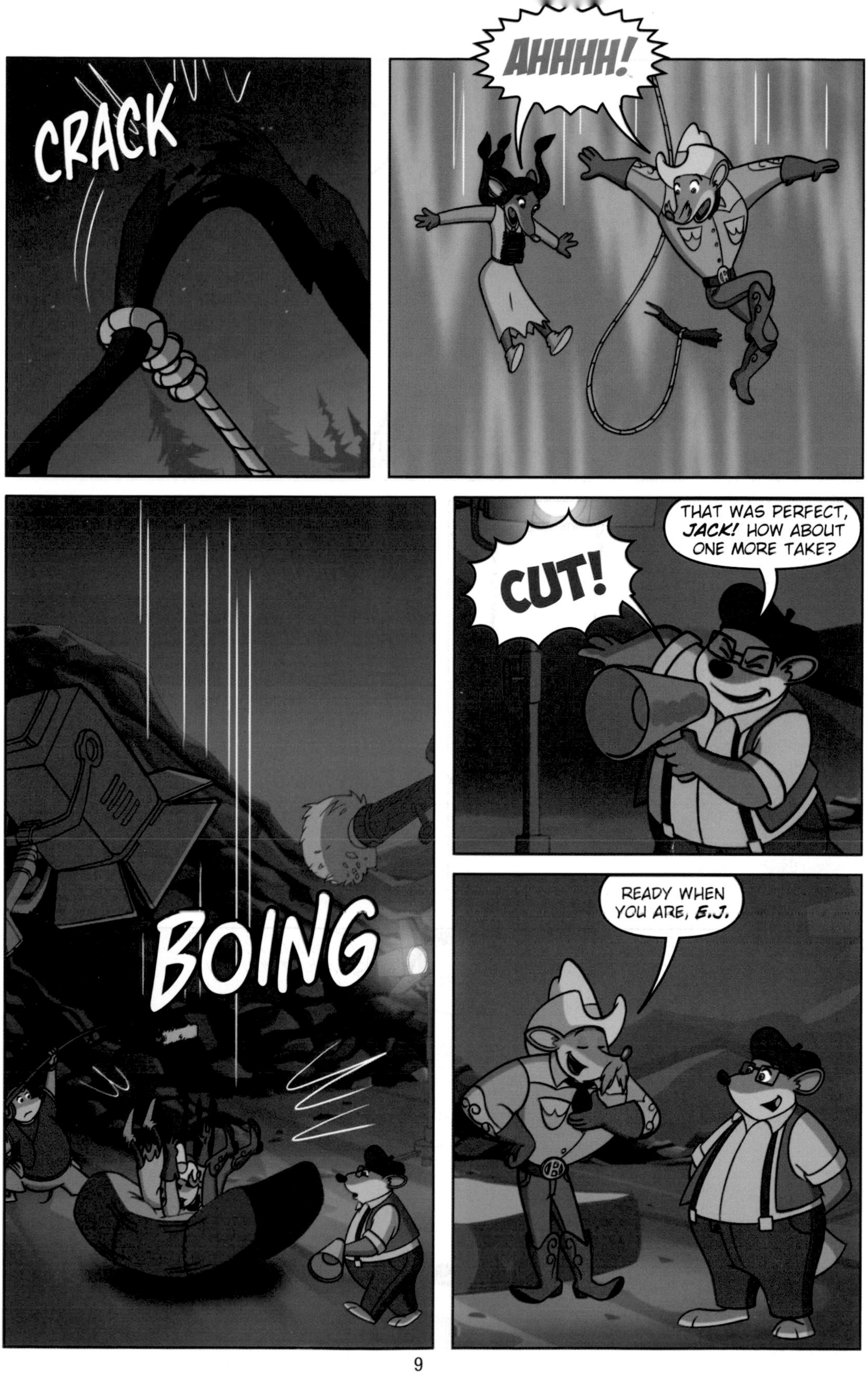
CRACK
AHHHH!
BOING
CUT!
THAT WAS PERFECT, JACK! HOW ABOUT ONE MORE TAKE?
READY WHEN YOU ARE, E.J.

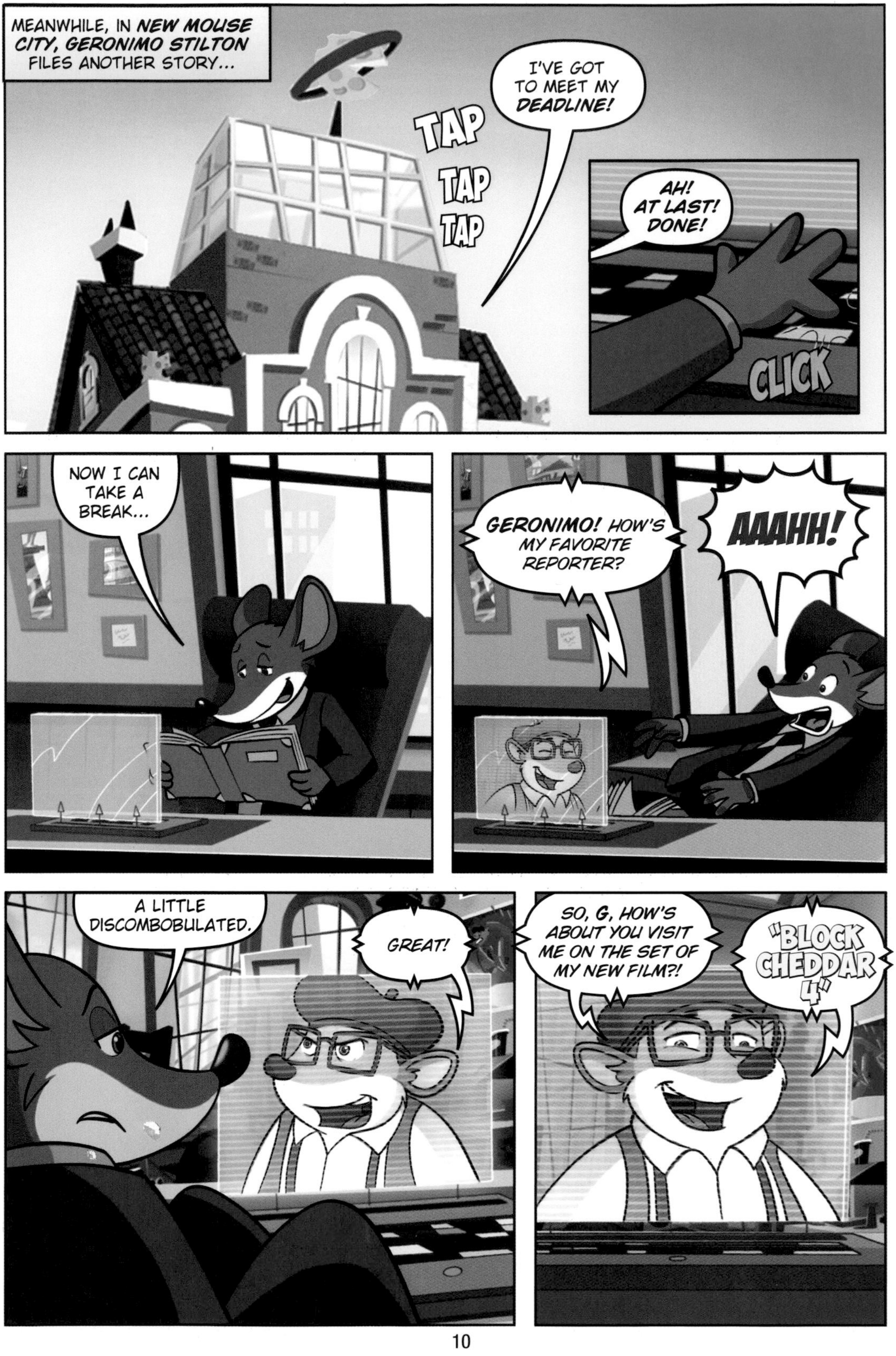

MEANWHILE, IN NEW MOUSE CITY, GERONIMO STILTON FILES ANOTHER STORY...
TAP TAP TAP
I'VE GOT TO MEET MY DEADLINE!
AH! AT LAST! DONE!
CLICK
NOW I CAN TAKE A BREAK...
GERONIMO! HOW'S MY FAVORITE REPORTER?
AAAHH!
A LITTLE DISCOMBOBULATED.
GREAT!
SO, G, HOW'S ABOUT YOU VISIT ME ON THE SET OF MY NEW FILM?!
"BLOCK CHEDDAR 4"

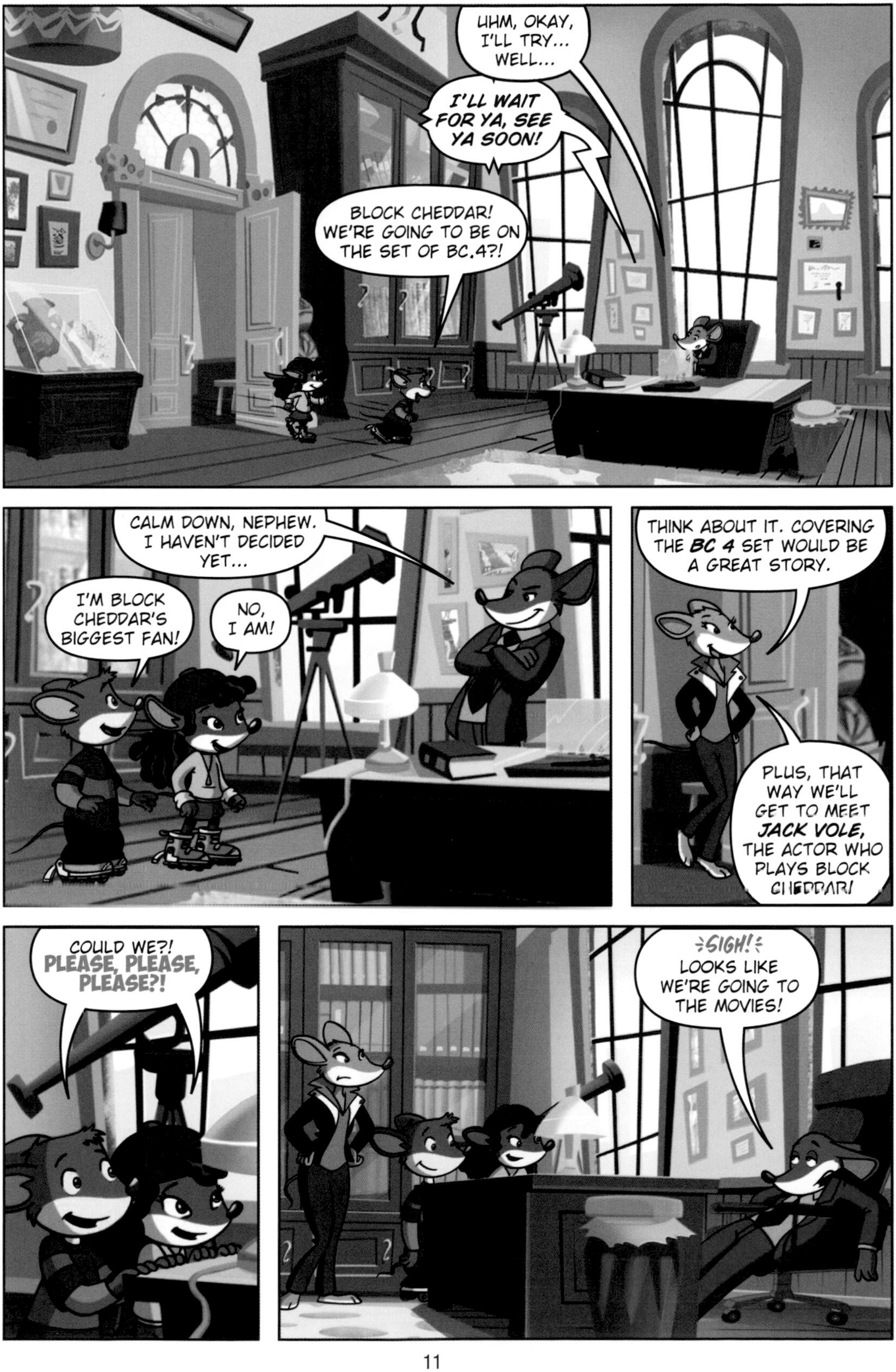
UHM, OKAY, I'LL TRY... WELL...
I'LL WAIT FOR YA, SEE YA SOON!
BLOCK CHEDDAR! WE'RE GOING TO BE ON THE SET OF BC.4?!
CALM DOWN, NEPHEW. I HAVEN'T DECIDED YET...
I'M BLOCK CHEDDAR'S BIGGEST FAN!
NO, I AM!
THINK ABOUT IT. COVERING THE BC 4 SET WOULD BE A GREAT STORY.
PLUS, THAT WAY WE'LL GET TO MEET JACK VOLE, THE ACTOR WHO PLAYS BLOCK CHEDDAR!
COULD WE?! PLEASE, PLEASE, PLEASE?!
SIGH!
LOOKS LIKE WE'RE GOING TO THE MOVIES!

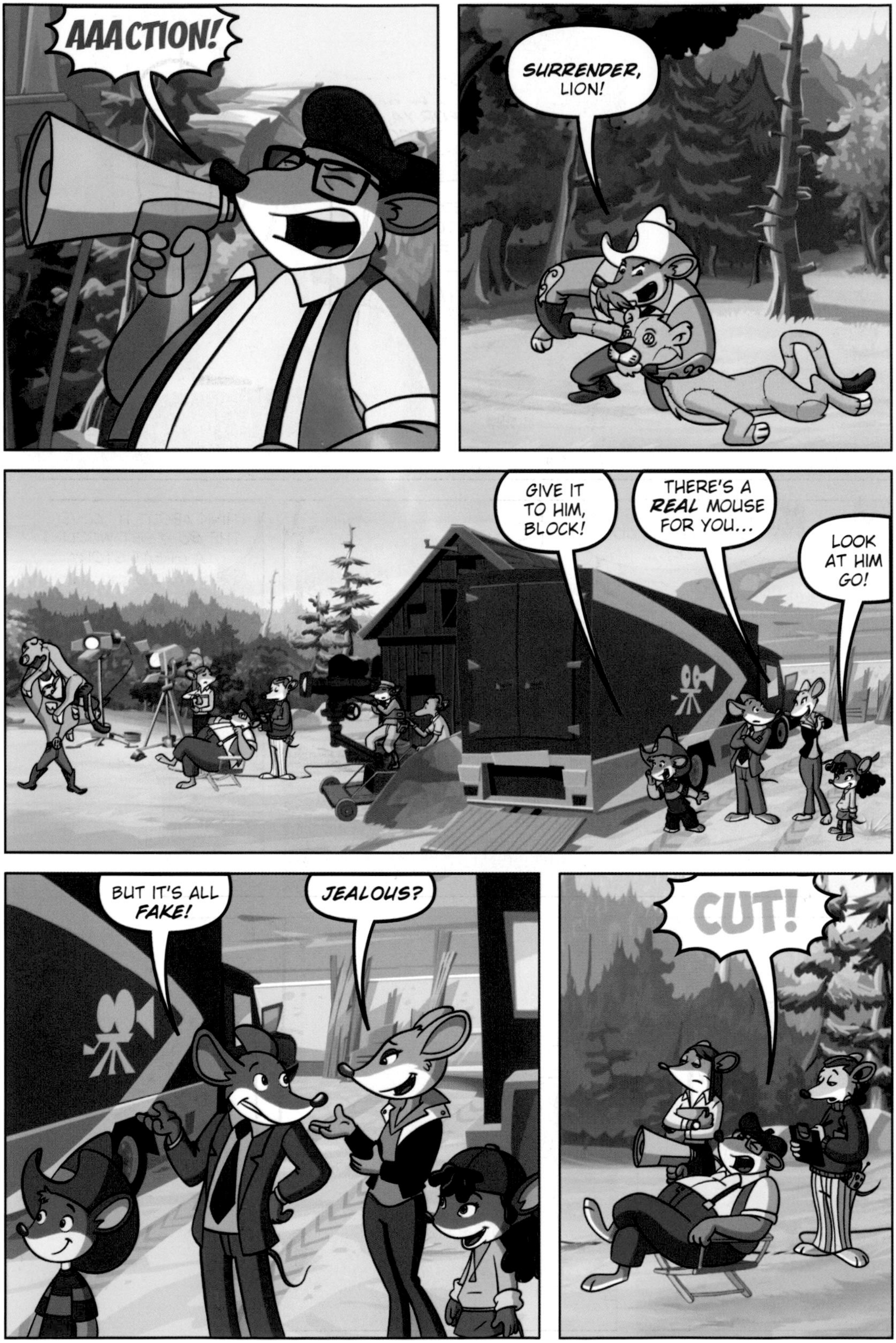
AAACTION!
SURRENDER, LION!
GIVE IT TO HIM, BLOCK!
THERE'S A REAL MOUSE FOR YOU...
LOOK AT HIM GO!
BUT IT'S ALL FAKE!
JEALOUS?
CUT!

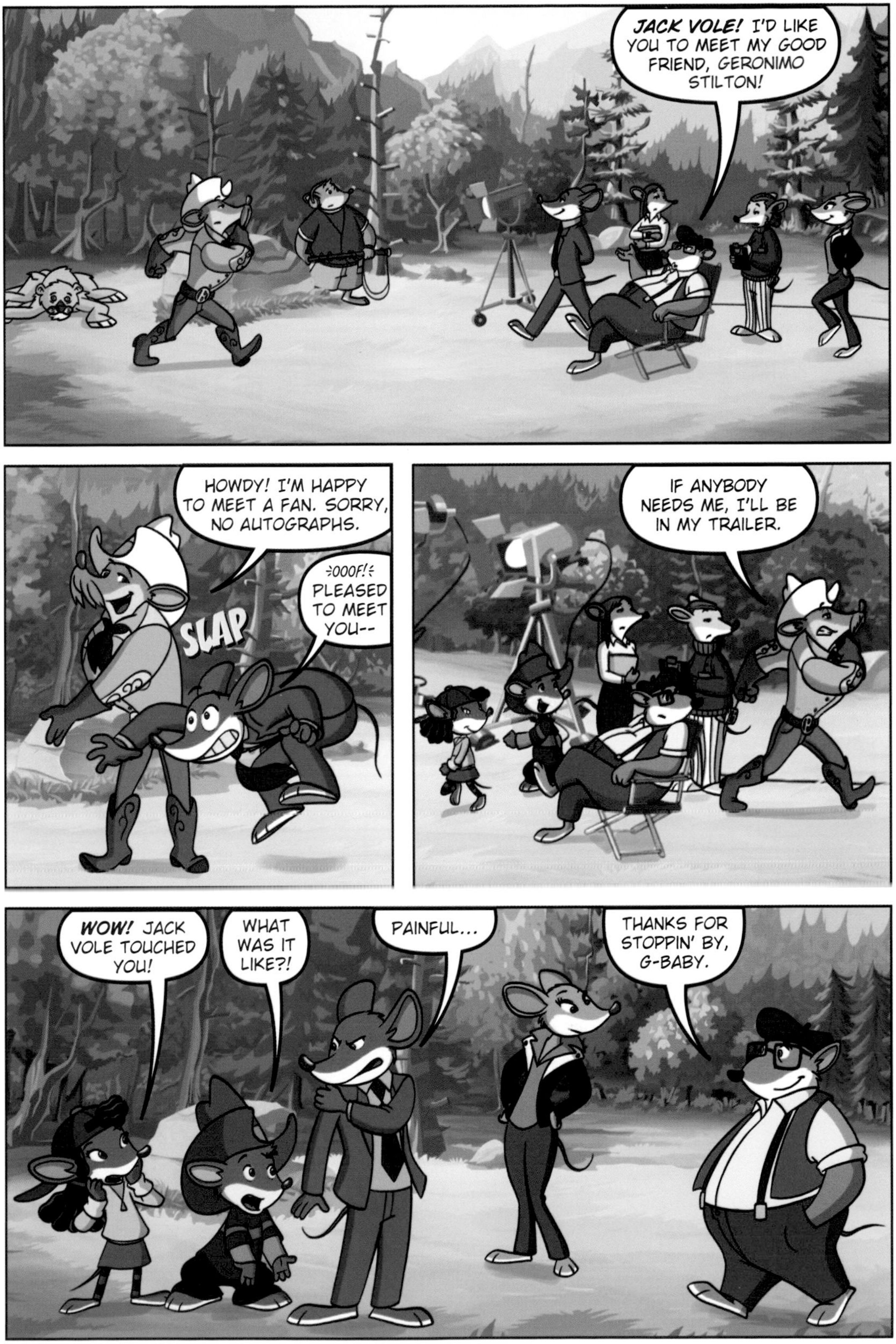
JACK VOLE! I'D LIKE YOU TO MEET MY GOOD FRIEND, GERONIMO STILTON!
HOWDY! I'M HAPPY TO MEET A FAN. SORRY, NO AUTOGRAPHS.
SLAP
OOOF! PLEASED TO MEET YOU--
IF ANYBODY NEEDS ME, I'LL BE IN MY TRAILER.
WOW! JACK VOLE TOUCHED YOU!
WHAT WAS IT LIKE?!
PAINFUL...
THANKS FOR STOPPIN' BY, G-BABY.

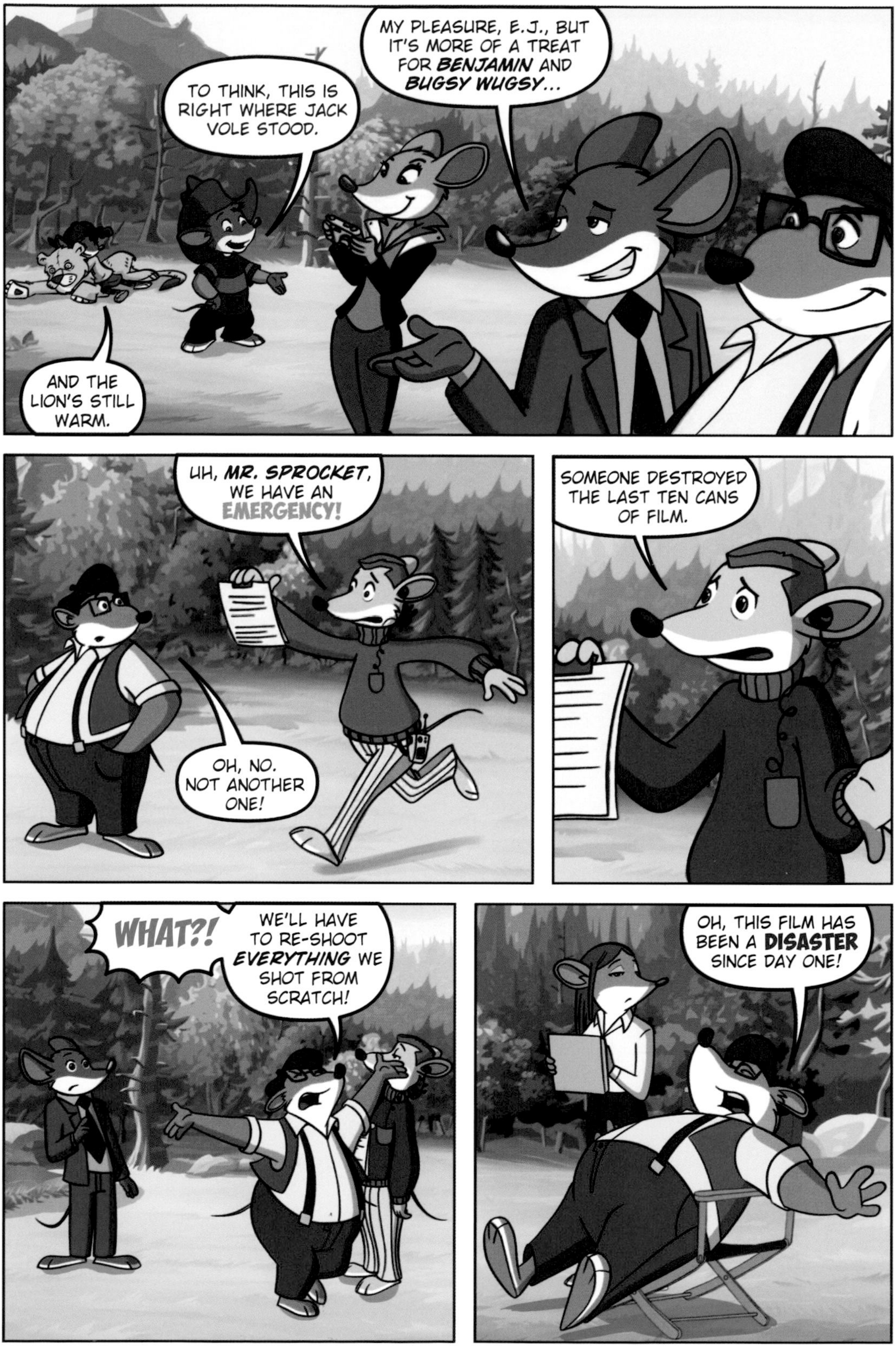
TO THINK, THIS IS RIGHT WHERE JACK VOLE STOOD.
AND THE LION'S STILL WARM.
MY PLEASURE, E.J., BUT IT'S MORE OF A TREAT FOR BENJAMIN AND BUGSY WUGSY...
UH, MR. SPROCKET, WE HAVE AN EMERGENCY!
OH, NO. NOT ANOTHER ONE!
SOMEONE DESTROYED THE LAST TEN CANS OF FILM.
WHAT?!
WE'LL HAVE TO RE-SHOOT EVERYTHING WE SHOT FROM SCRATCH!
OH, THIS FILM HAS BEEN A DISASTER SINCE DAY ONE!

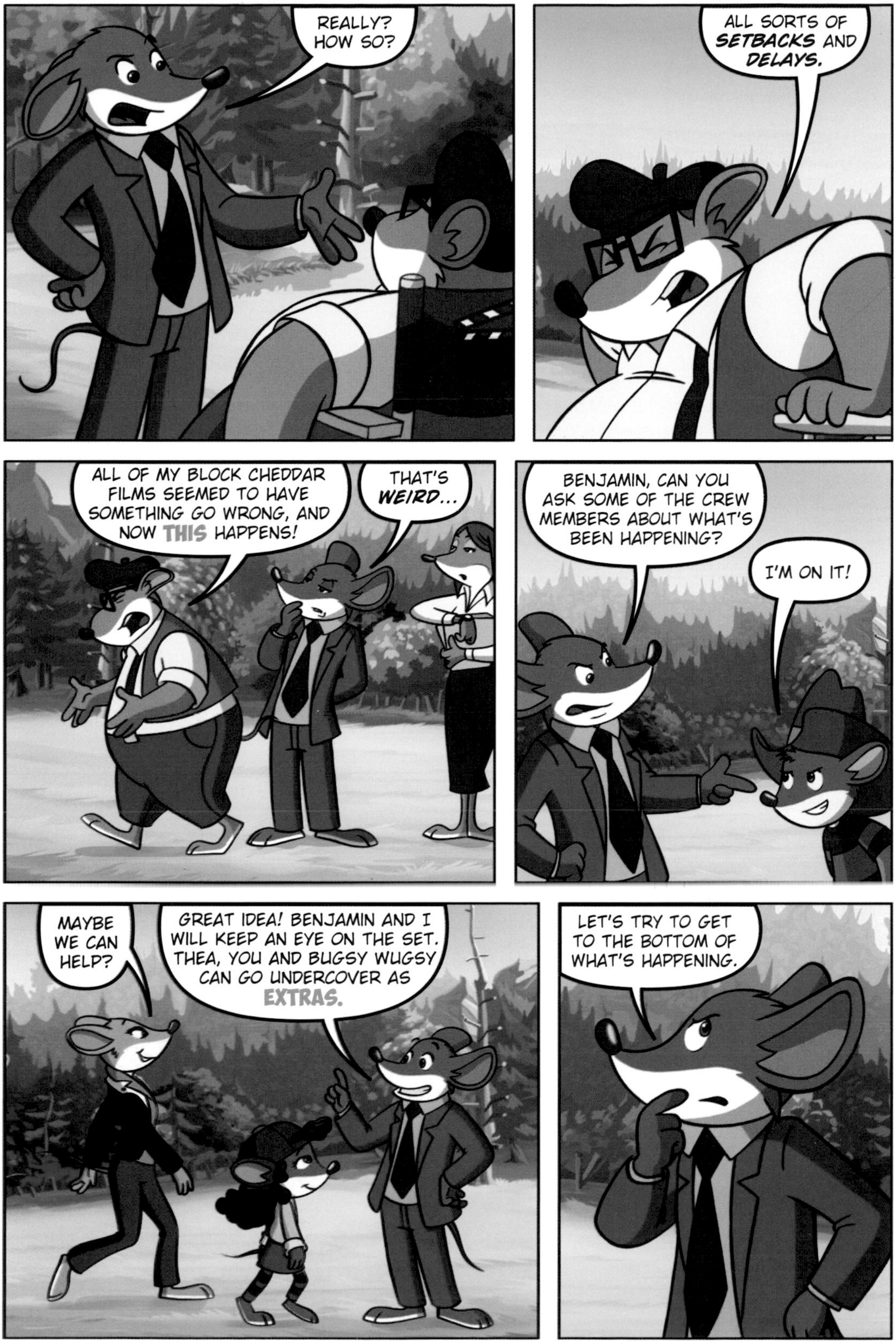
REALLY? HOW SO?
ALL SORTS OF SETBACKS AND DELAYS.
ALL OF MY BLOCK CHEDDAR FILMS SEEMED TO HAVE SOMETHING GO WRONG, AND NOW THIS HAPPENS!
THAT'S WEIRD...
BENJAMIN, CAN YOU ASK SOME OF THE CREW MEMBERS ABOUT WHAT'S BEEN HAPPENING?
I'M ON IT!
MAYBE WE CAN HELP?
GREAT IDEA! BENJAMIN AND I WILL KEEP AN EYE ON THE SET. THEA, YOU AND BUGSY WUGSY CAN GO UNDERCOVER AS EXTRAS.
LET'S TRY TO GET TO THE BOTTOM OF WHAT'S HAPPENING.

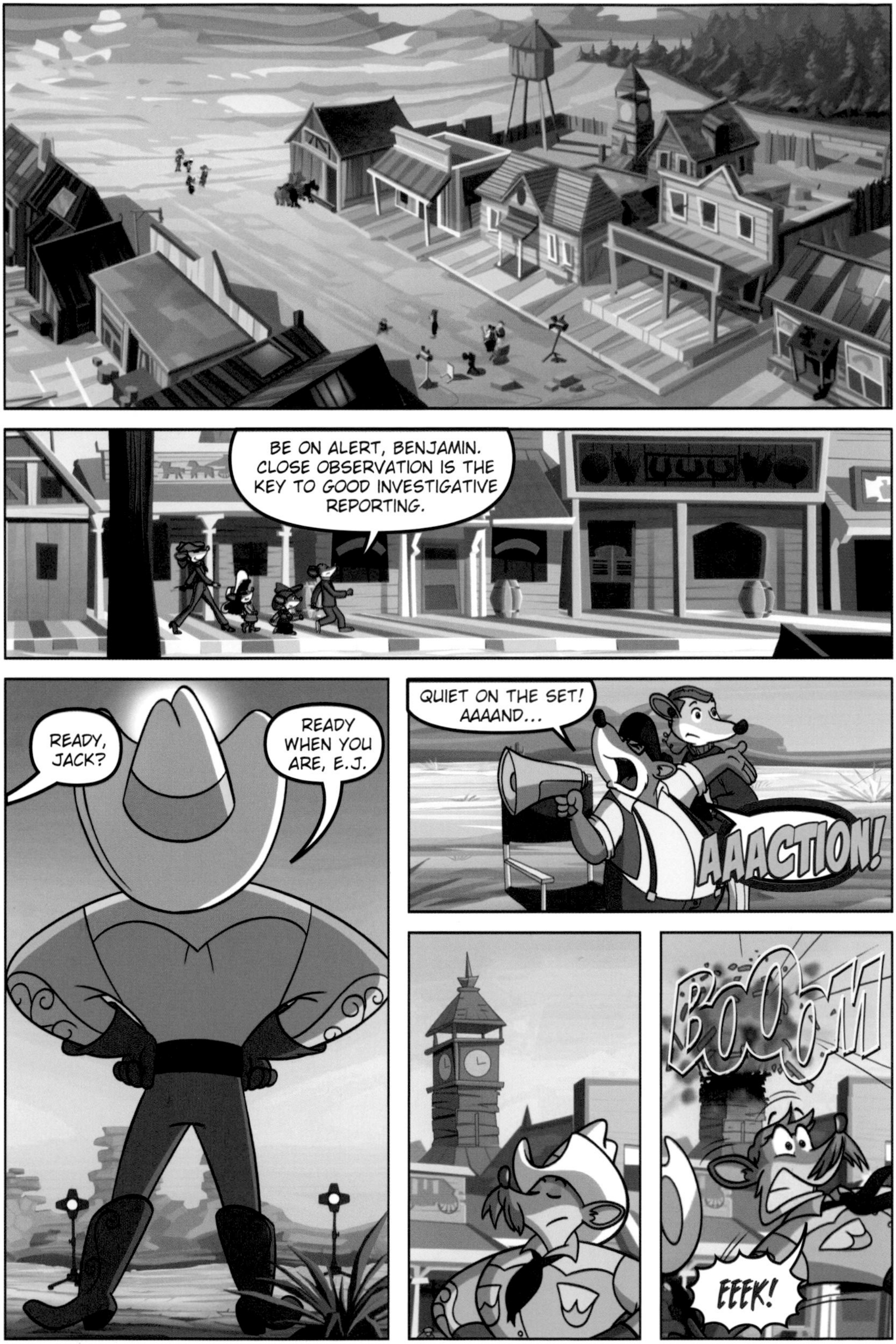
BE ON ALERT, BENJAMIN. CLOSE OBSERVATION IS THE KEY TO GOOD INVESTIGATIVE REPORTING.
READY, JACK?
READY WHEN YOU ARE, E.J.
QUIET ON THE SET! AAAAND...
AAACTION!
BOOOM
EEEK!

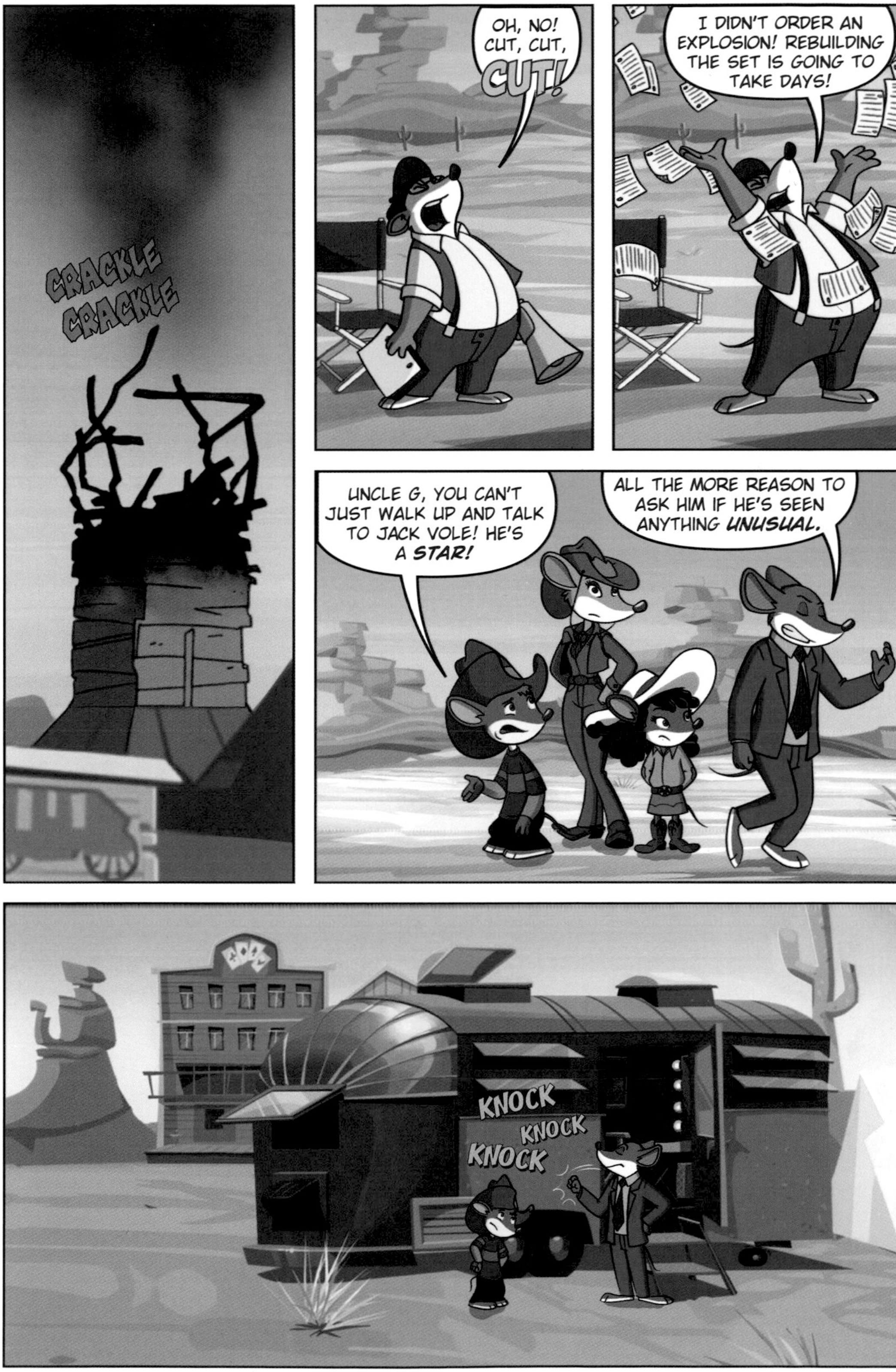
CRACKLE
CRACKLE
OH, NO! CUT, CUT, CUT!
I DIDN'T ORDER AN EXPLOSION! REBUILDING THE SET IS GOING TO TAKE DAYS!
UNCLE G, YOU CAN'T JUST WALK UP AND TALK TO JACK VOLE! HE'S A STAR!
ALL THE MORE REASON TO ASK HIM IF HE'S SEEN ANYTHING UNUSUAL.
KNOCK
KNOCK
KNOCK

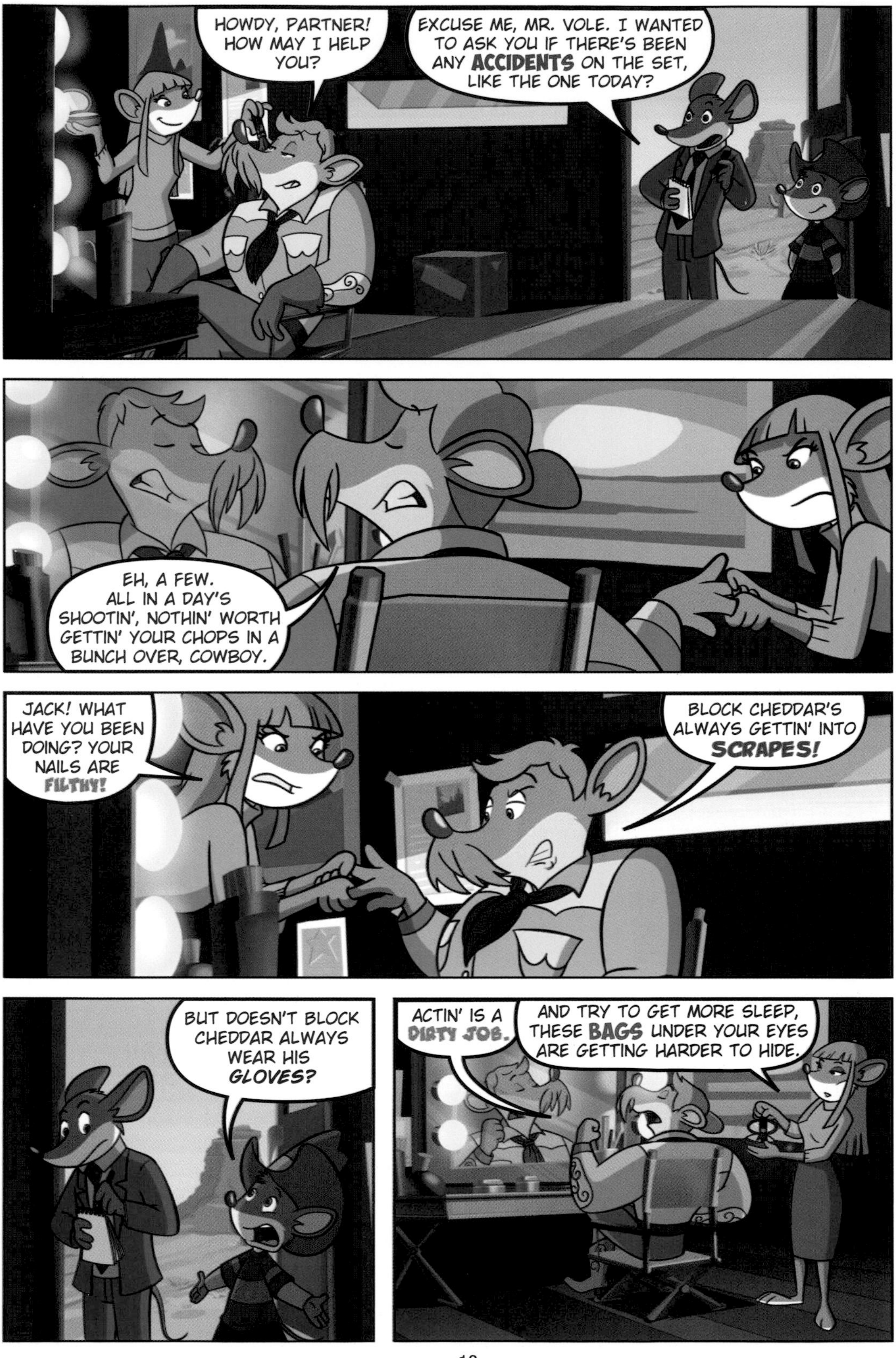
HOWDY, PARTNER! HOW MAY I HELP YOU?
EXCUSE ME, MR. VOLE. I WANTED TO ASK YOU IF THERE'S BEEN ANY ACCIDENTS ON THE SET, LIKE THE ONE TODAY?
EH, A FEW. ALL IN A DAY'S SHOOTIN', NOTHIN' WORTH GETTIN' YOUR CHOPS IN A BUNCH OVER, COWBOY.
JACK! WHAT HAVE YOU BEEN DOING? YOUR NAILS ARE FILTHY!
BLOCK CHEDDAR'S ALWAYS GETTIN' INTO SCRAPES!
BUT DOESN'T BLOCK CHEDDAR ALWAYS WEAR HIS GLOVES?
ACTIN' IS A DIRTY JOB.
AND TRY TO GET MORE SLEEP, THESE BAGS UNDER YOUR EYES ARE GETTING HARDER TO HIDE.

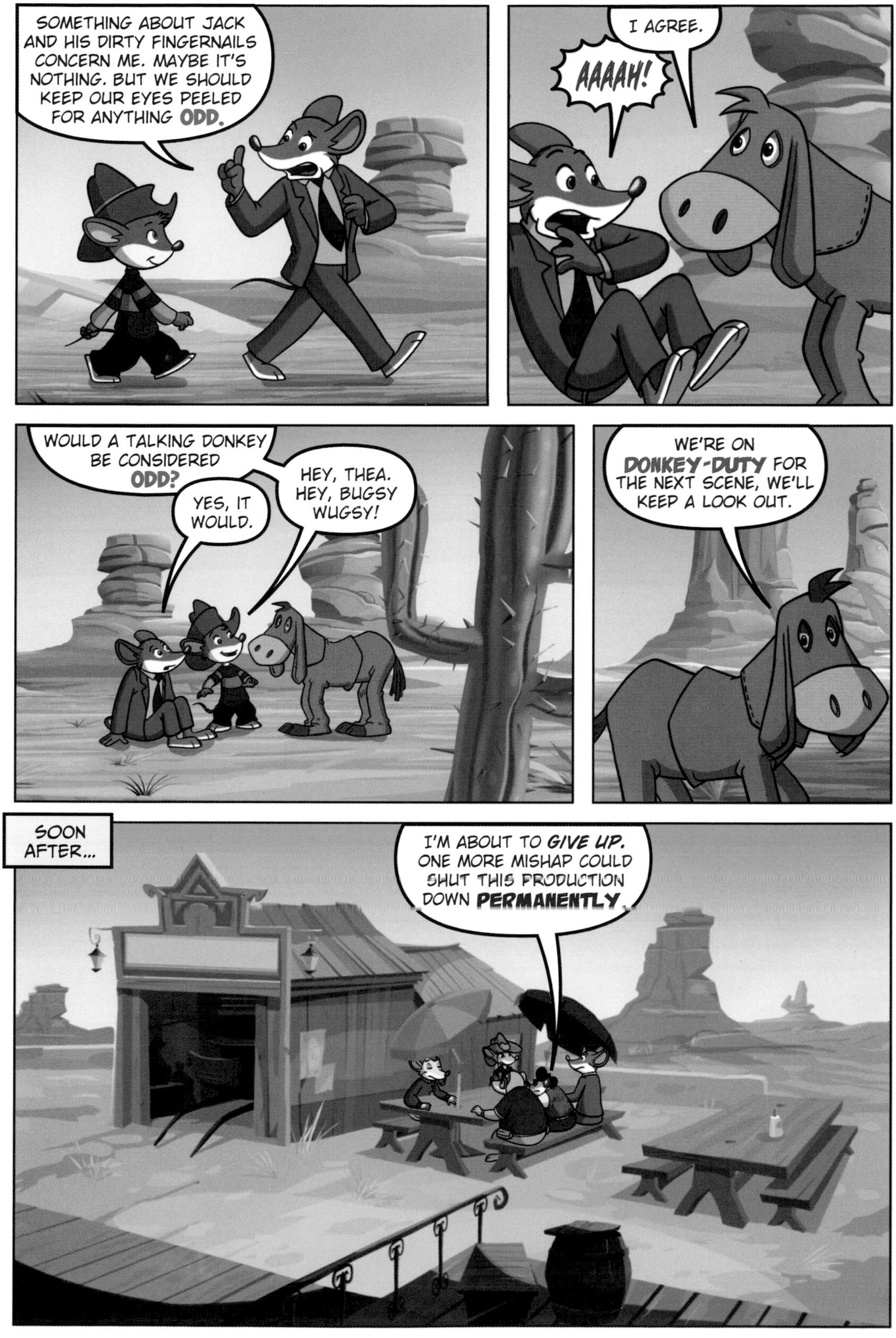
SOMETHING ABOUT JACK AND HIS DIRTY FINGERNAILS CONCERN ME. MAYBE IT'S NOTHING. BUT WE SHOULD KEEP OUR EYES PEELED FOR ANYTHING ODD.
I AGREE.
AAAAH!
WOULD A TALKING DONKEY BE CONSIDERED ODD?
YES, IT WOULD.
HEY, THEA. HEY, BUGSY WUGSY!
WE'RE ON DONKEY-DUTY FOR THE NEXT SCENE, WE'LL KEEP A LOOK OUT.
SOON AFTER...
I'M ABOUT TO GIVE UP. ONE MORE MISHAP COULD SHUT THIS PRODUCTION DOWN PERMANENTLY.

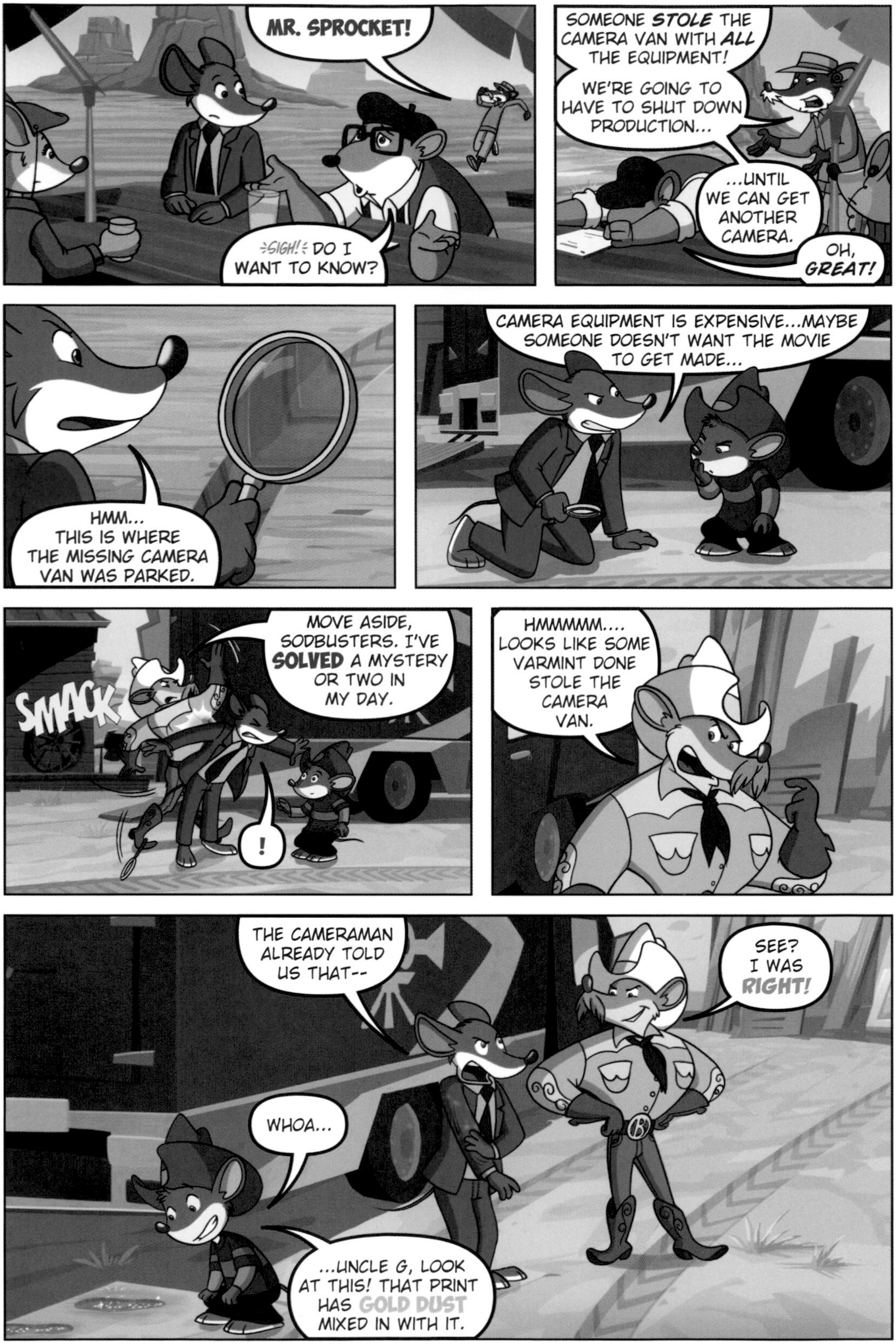
MR. SPROCKET!
SIGH! DO I WANT TO KNOW?
SOMEONE STOLE THE CAMERA VAN WITH ALL THE EQUIPMENT!
WE'RE GOING TO HAVE TO SHUT DOWN PRODUCTION...
...UNTIL WE CAN GET ANOTHER CAMERA.
OH, GREAT!
HMM... THIS IS WHERE THE MISSING CAMERA VAN WAS PARKED.
CAMERA EQUIPMENT IS EXPENSIVE...MAYBE SOMEONE DOESN'T WANT THE MOVIE TO GET MADE...
MOVE ASIDE, SODBUSTERS. I'VE SOLVED A MYSTERY OR TWO IN MY DAY.
SMACK
!
HMMMMM.... LOOKS LIKE SOME VARMINT DONE STOLE THE CAMERA VAN.
THE CAMERAMAN ALREADY TOLD US THAT--
SEE? I WAS RIGHT!
WHOA...
...UNCLE G, LOOK AT THIS! THAT PRINT HAS GOLD DUST MIXED IN WITH IT.

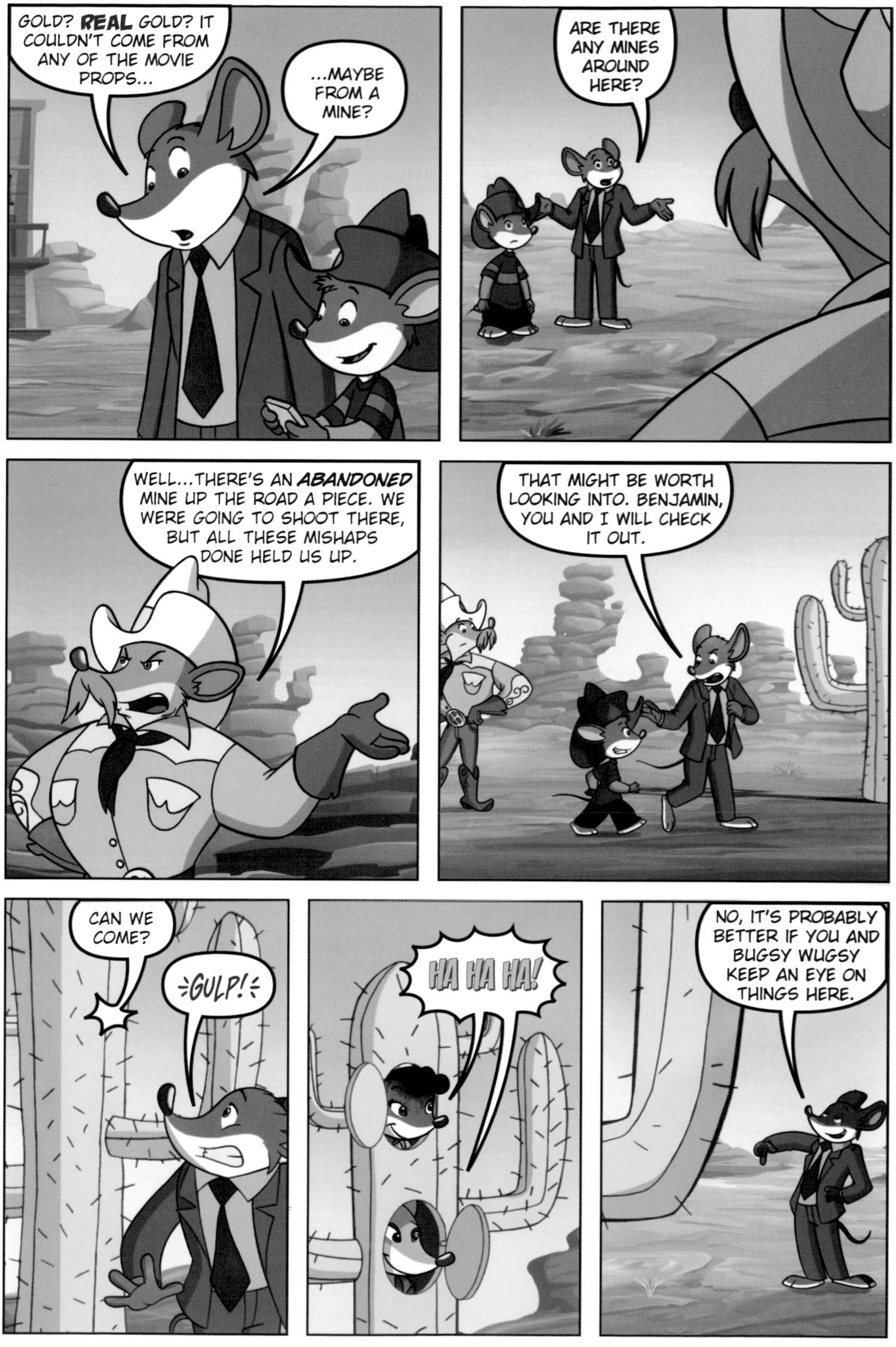

GOLD? **REAL** GOLD? IT COULDN'T COME FROM ANY OF THE MOVIE PROPS...
...MAYBE FROM A MINE?
ARE THERE ANY MINES AROUND HERE?
WELL...THERE'S AN ***ABANDONED*** MINE UP THE ROAD A PIECE. WE WERE GOING TO SHOOT THERE, BUT ALL THESE MISHAPS DONE HELD US UP.
THAT MIGHT BE WORTH LOOKING INTO. BENJAMIN, YOU AND I WILL CHECK IT OUT.
CAN WE COME?
GULP!
HA HA HA!
NO, IT'S PROBABLY BETTER IF YOU AND BUGSY WUGSY KEEP AN EYE ON THINGS HERE.

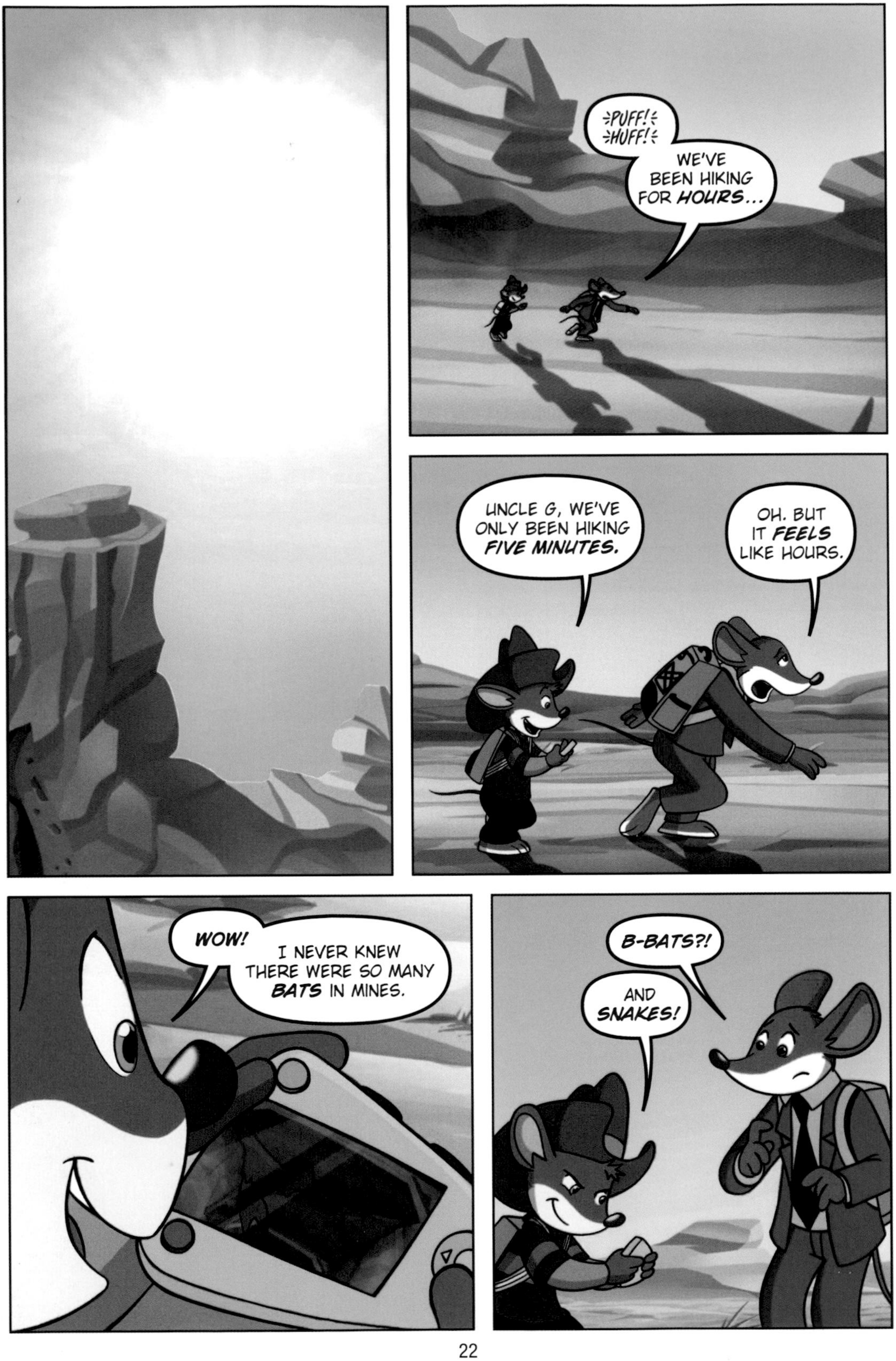
PUFF! HUFF!
WE'VE BEEN HIKING FOR HOURS...
UNCLE G, WE'VE ONLY BEEN HIKING FIVE MINUTES.
OH. BUT IT FEELS LIKE HOURS.
WOW!
I NEVER KNEW THERE WERE SO MANY BATS IN MINES.
B-BATS?!
AND SNAKES!

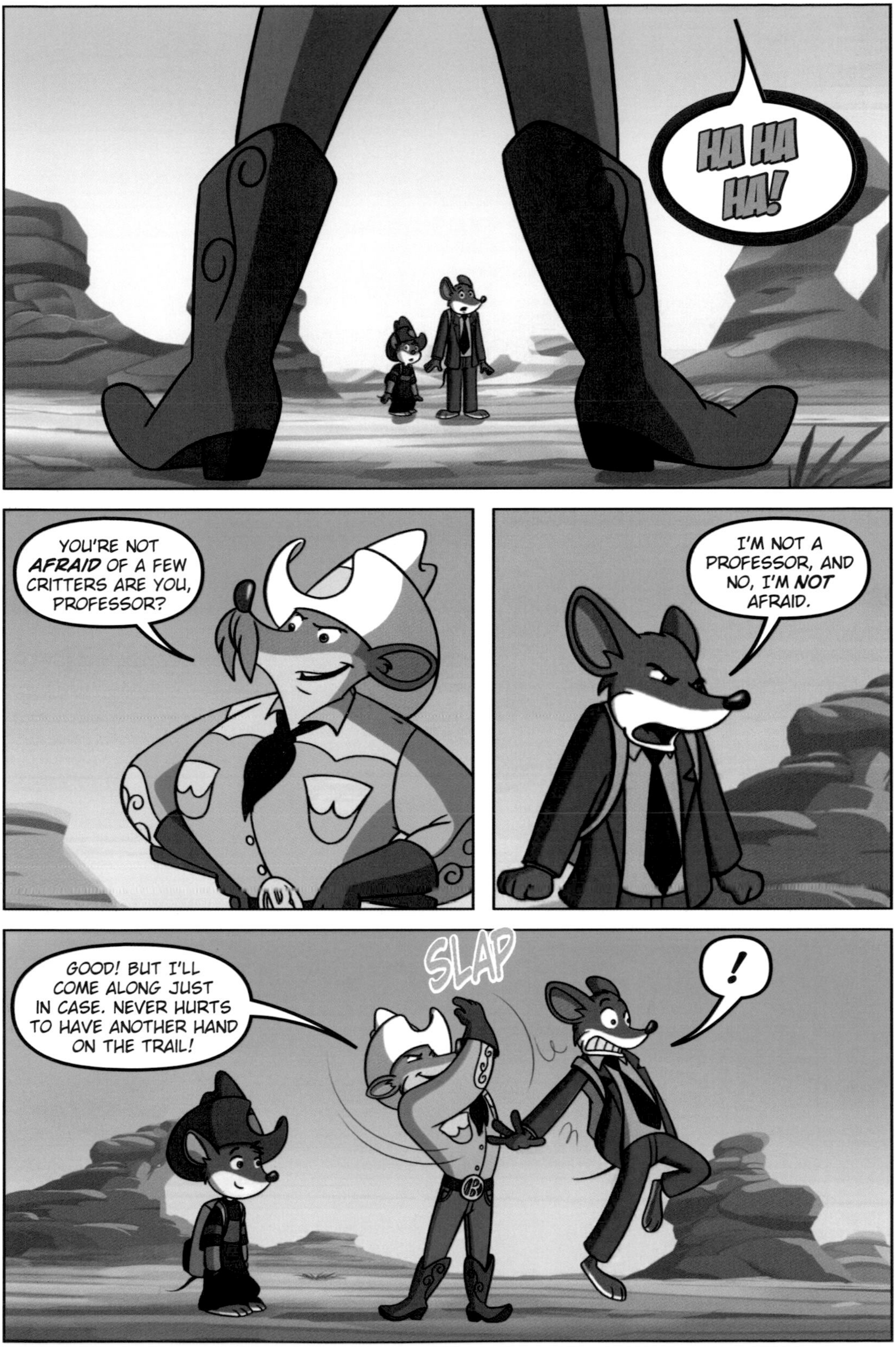
HA HA HA!
YOU'RE NOT AFRAID OF A FEW CRITTERS ARE YOU, PROFESSOR?
I'M NOT A PROFESSOR, AND NO, I'M NOT AFRAID.
GOOD! BUT I'LL COME ALONG JUST IN CASE. NEVER HURTS TO HAVE ANOTHER HAND ON THE TRAIL!
SLAP
!

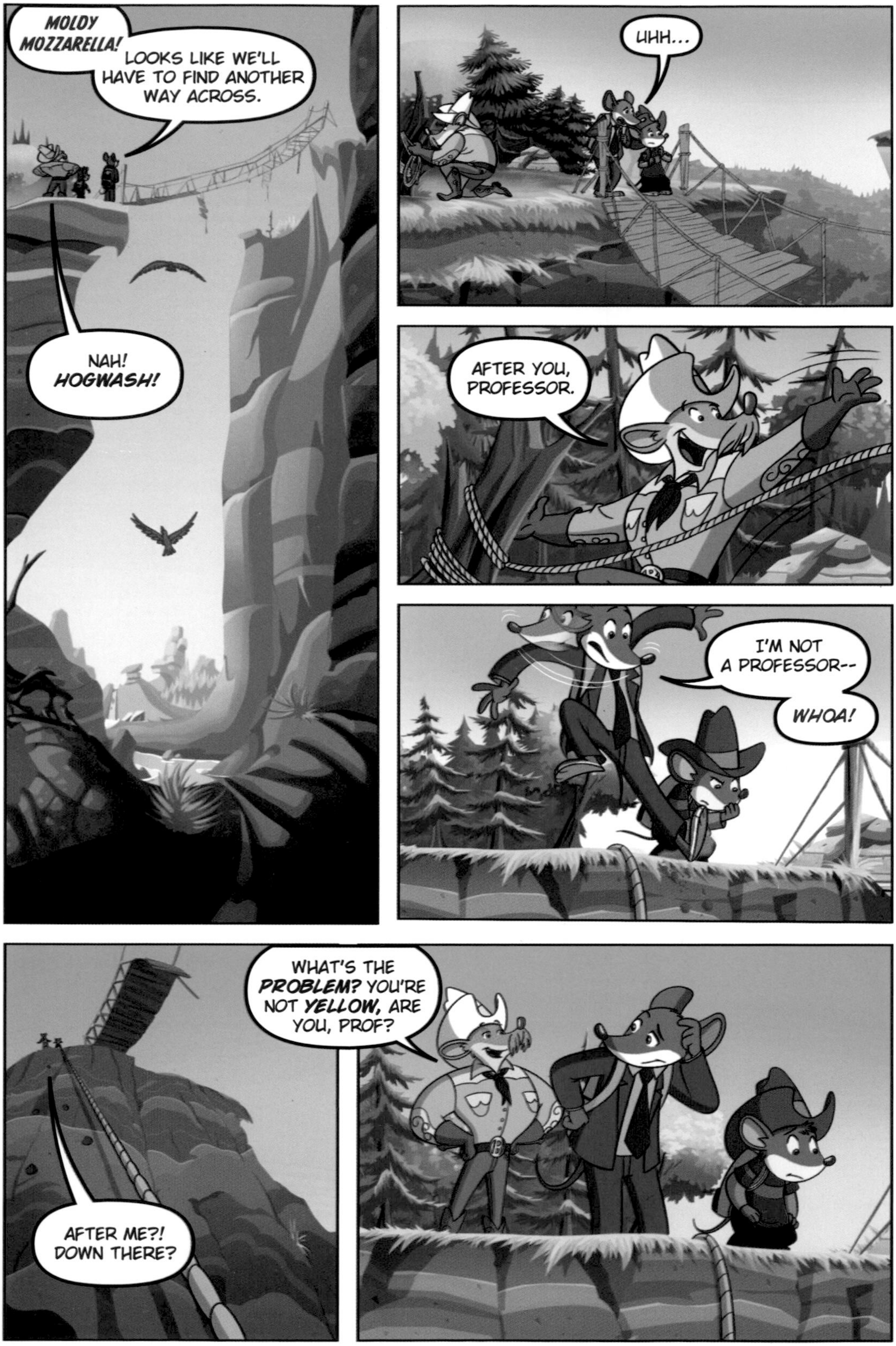
MOLDY MOZZARELLA!
LOOKS LIKE WE'LL HAVE TO FIND ANOTHER WAY ACROSS.
NAH! HOGWASH!
UHH...
AFTER YOU, PROFESSOR.
I'M NOT A PROFESSOR--
WHOA!
AFTER ME?! DOWN THERE?
WHAT'S THE PROBLEM? YOU'RE NOT YELLOW, ARE YOU, PROF?

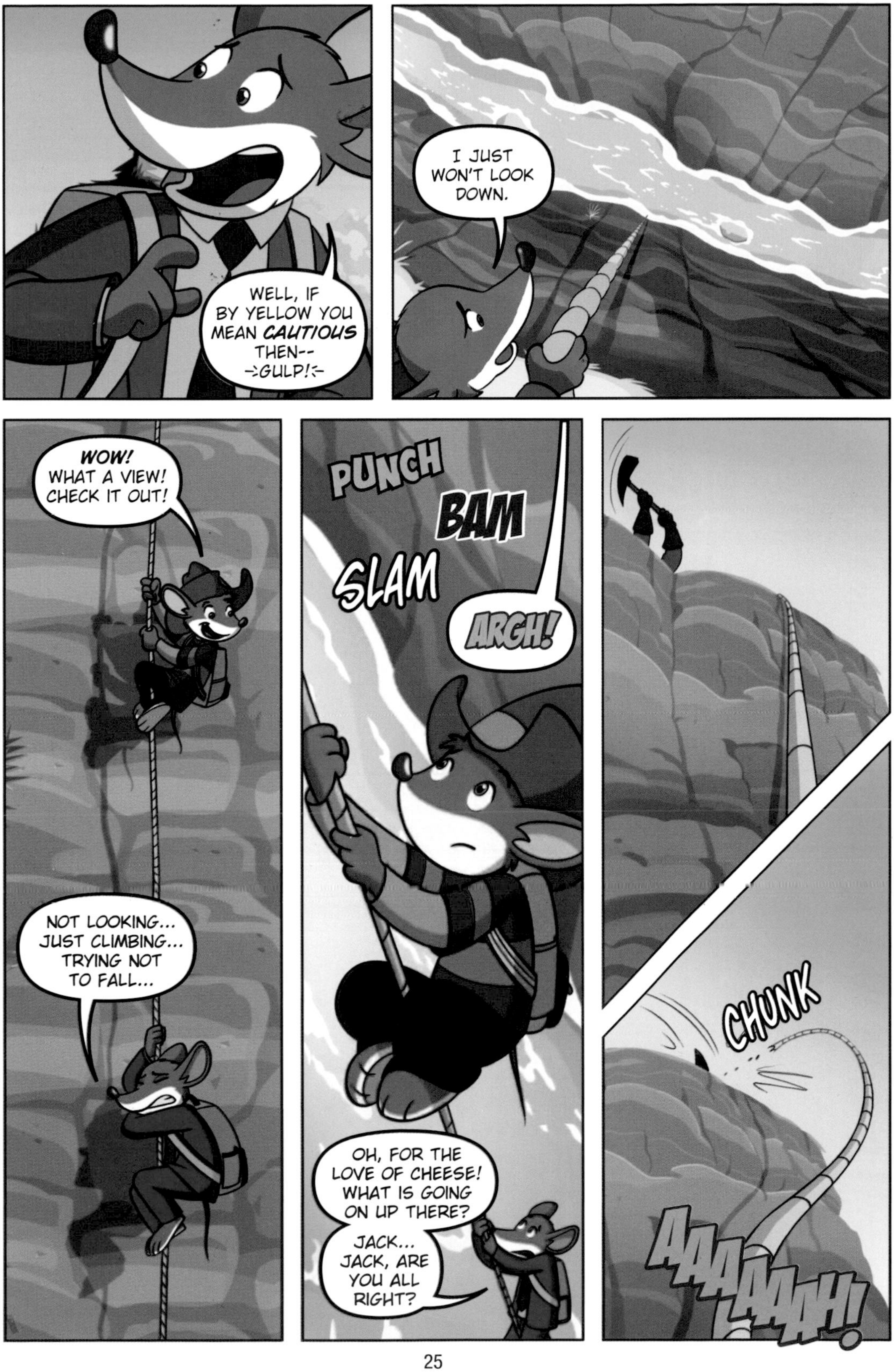
WELL, IF BY YELLOW YOU MEAN ***CAUTIOUS*** THEN-- -GULP!-
I JUST WON'T LOOK DOWN.
WOW! WHAT A VIEW! CHECK IT OUT!
NOT LOOKING... JUST CLIMBING... TRYING NOT TO FALL...
PUNCH
BAM
SLAM
ARGH!
OH, FOR THE LOVE OF CHEESE! WHAT IS GOING ON UP THERE?
JACK... JACK, ARE YOU ALL RIGHT?
CHUNK
AAAAAAAH!

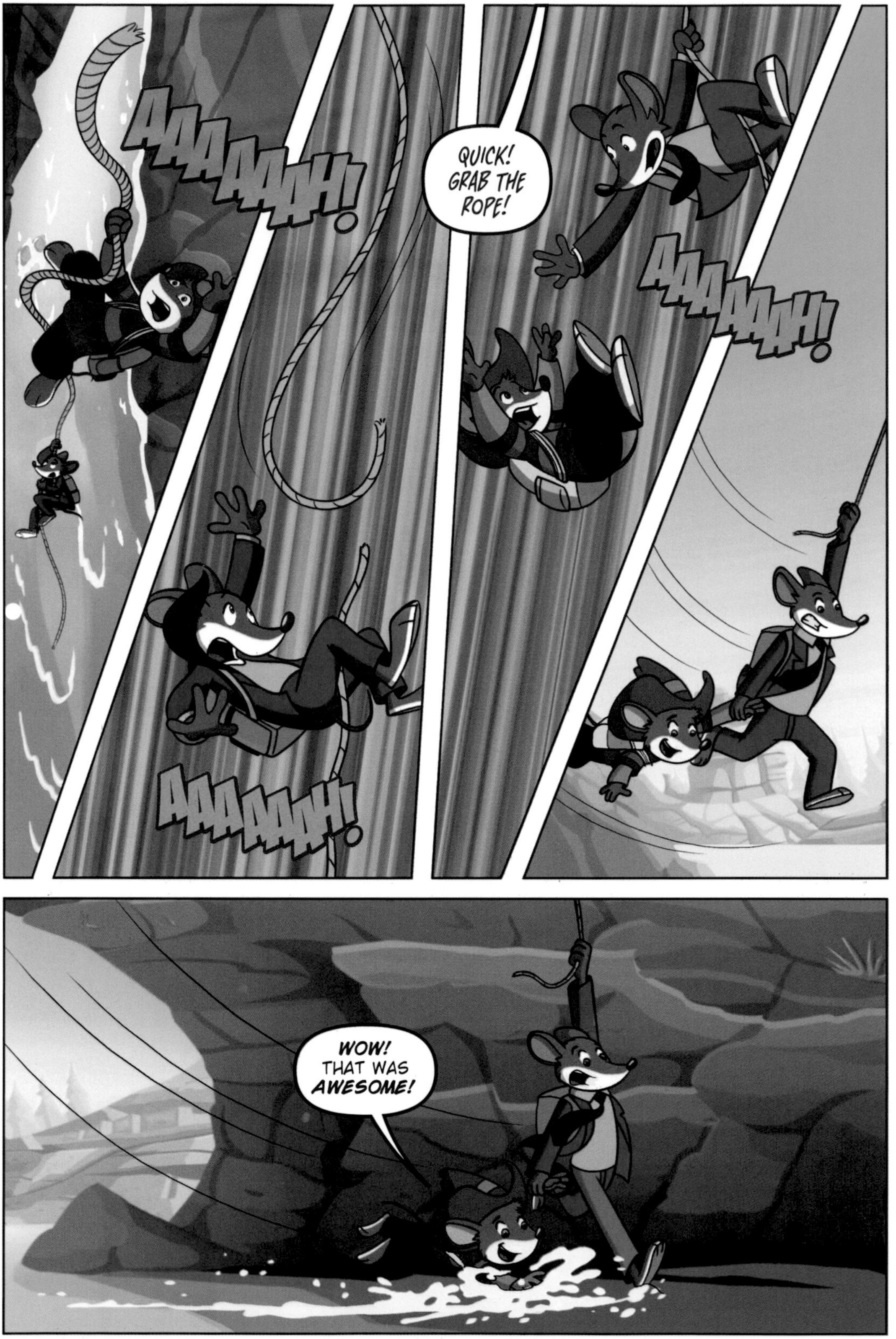
AAAAAAAH!
AAAAAAH!
QUICK! GRAB THE ROPE!
AAAAAAAH!
WOW! THAT WAS AWESOME!

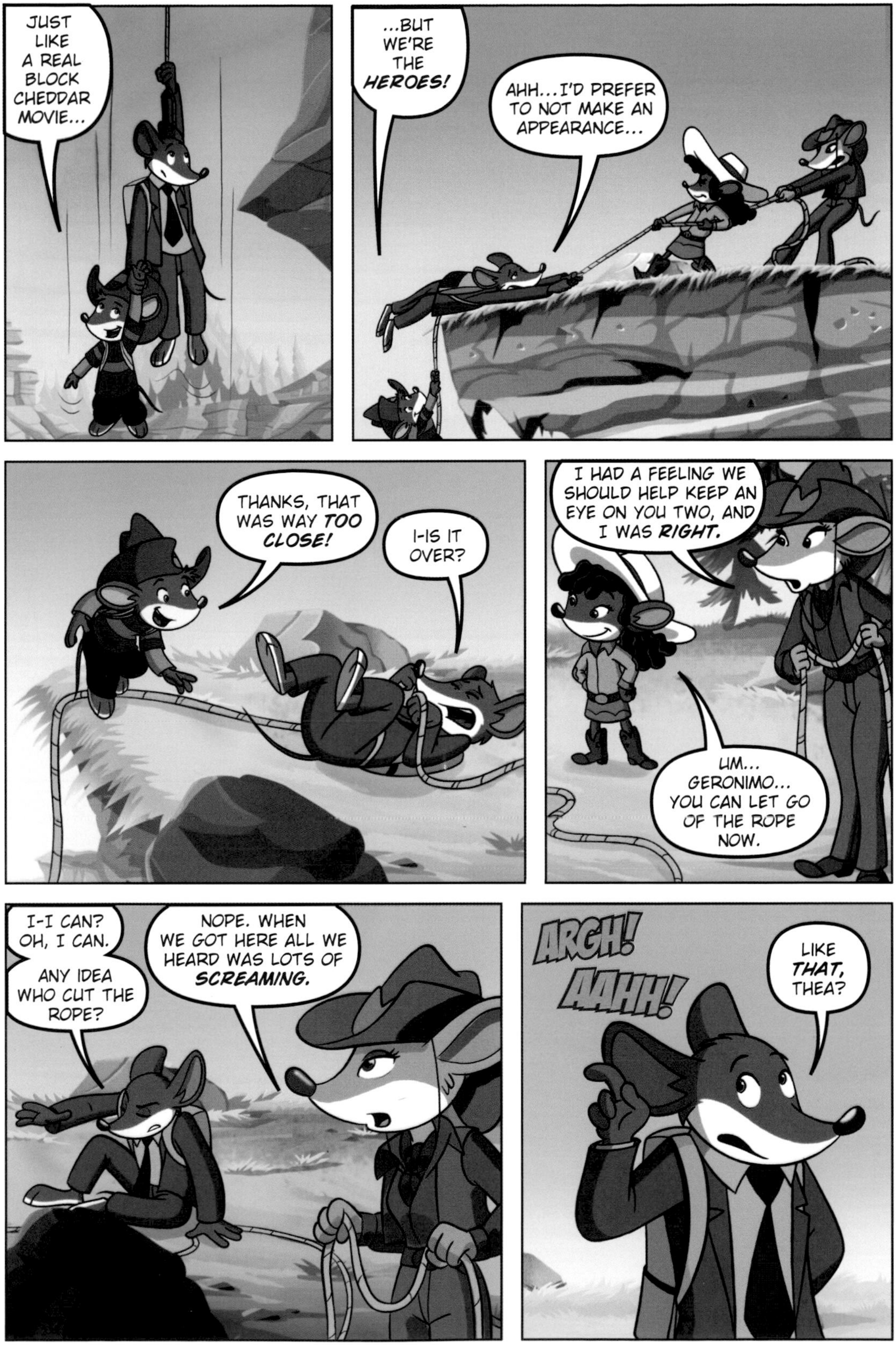
JUST LIKE A REAL BLOCK CHEDDAR MOVIE...
...BUT WE'RE THE HEROES!
AHH...I'D PREFER TO NOT MAKE AN APPEARANCE...
THANKS, THAT WAS WAY TOO CLOSE!
I-IS IT OVER?
I HAD A FEELING WE SHOULD HELP KEEP AN EYE ON YOU TWO, AND I WAS RIGHT.
UM... GERONIMO... YOU CAN LET GO OF THE ROPE NOW.
I-I CAN? OH, I CAN.
ANY IDEA WHO CUT THE ROPE?
NOPE. WHEN WE GOT HERE ALL WE HEARD WAS LOTS OF SCREAMING.
ARGH!
AAHH!
LIKE THAT, THEA?

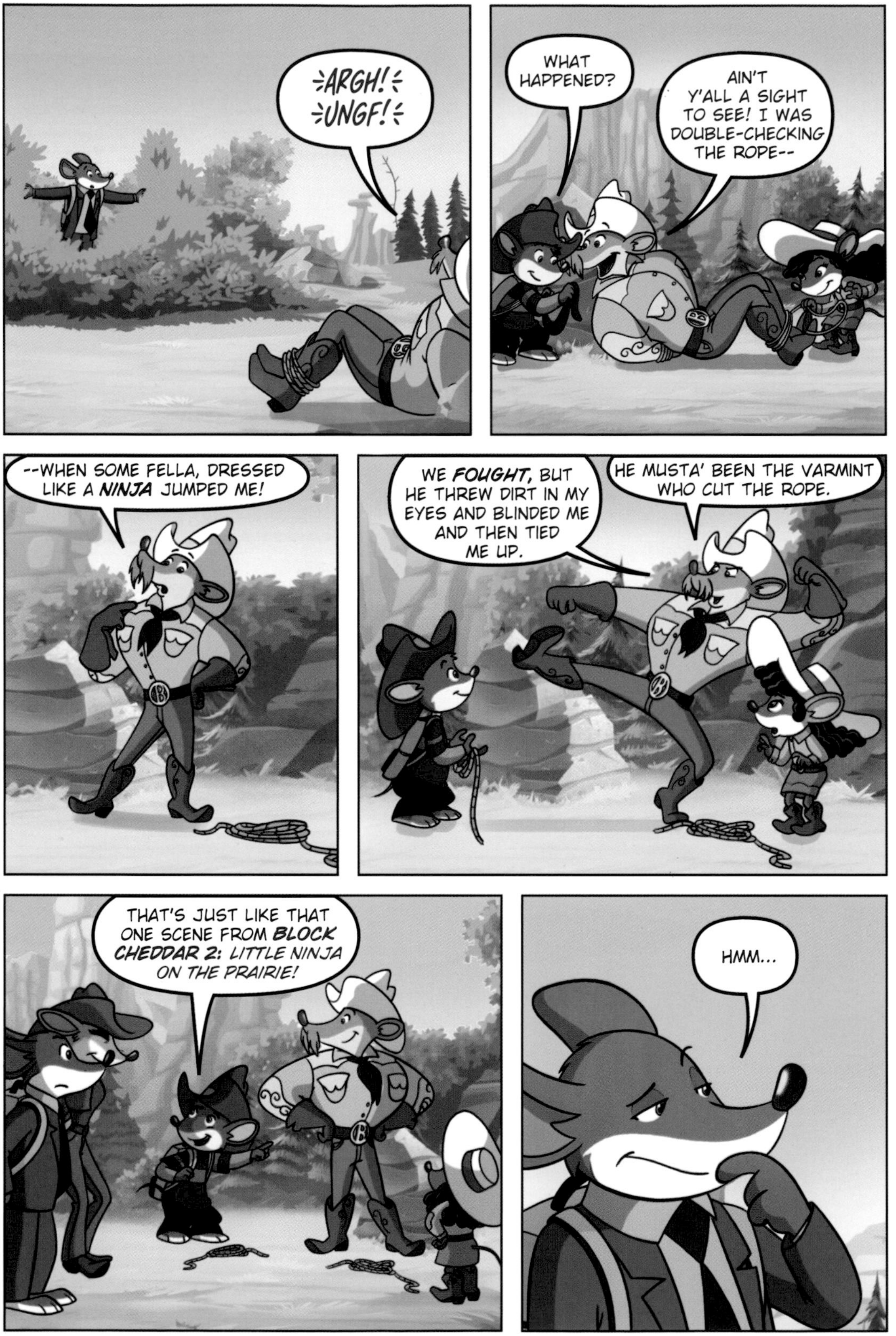
ARGH!
UNGF!
WHAT HAPPENED?
AIN'T Y'ALL A SIGHT TO SEE! I WAS DOUBLE-CHECKING THE ROPE--
--WHEN SOME FELLA, DRESSED LIKE A NINJA JUMPED ME!
WE FOUGHT, BUT HE THREW DIRT IN MY EYES AND BLINDED ME AND THEN TIED ME UP.
HE MUSTA' BEEN THE VARMINT WHO CUT THE ROPE.
THAT'S JUST LIKE THAT ONE SCENE FROM BLOCK CHEDDAR 2: LITTLE NINJA ON THE PRAIRIE!
HMM...

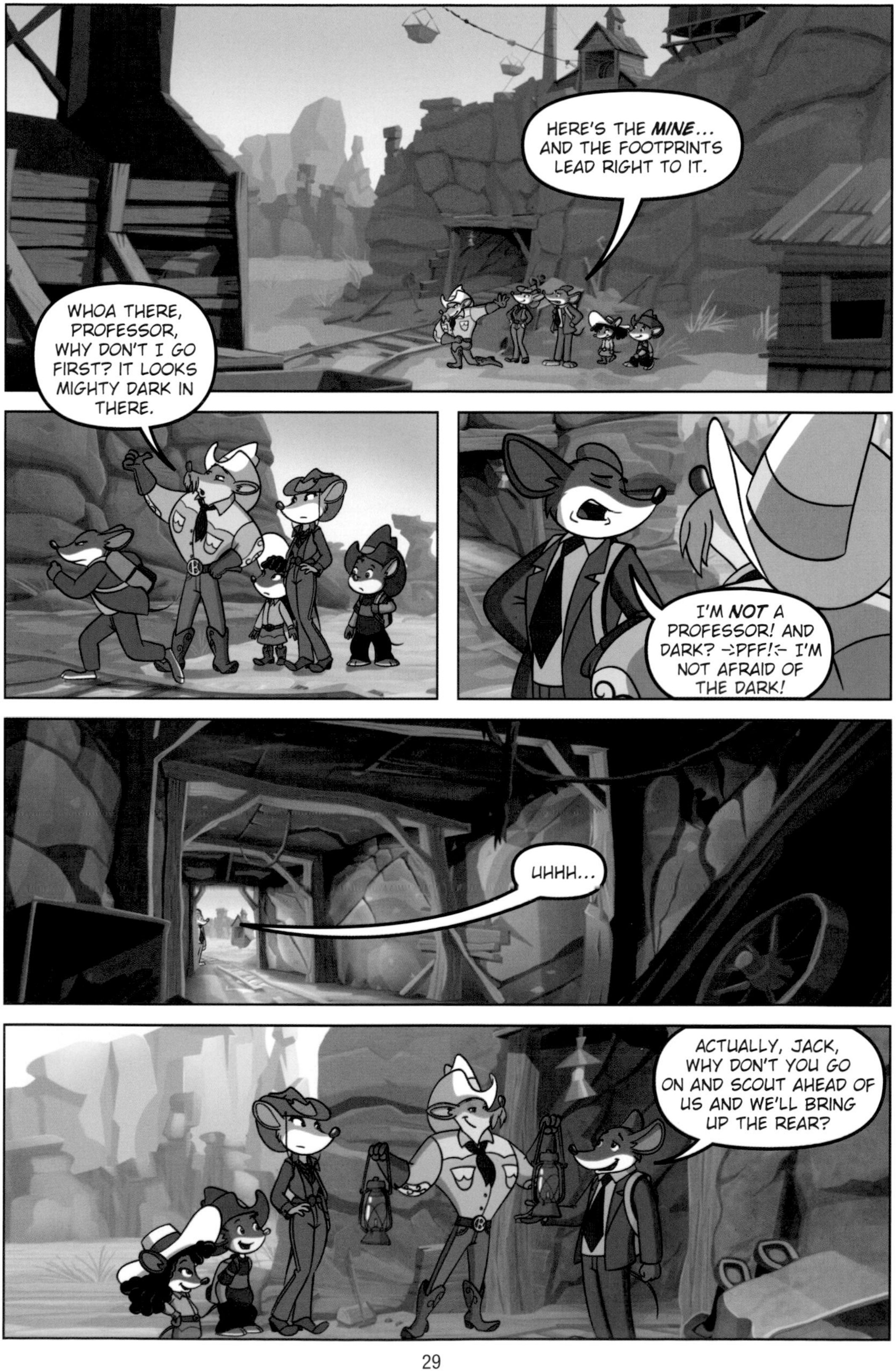
HERE'S THE *MINE*... AND THE FOOTPRINTS LEAD RIGHT TO IT.
WHOA THERE, PROFESSOR, WHY DON'T I GO FIRST? IT LOOKS MIGHTY DARK IN THERE.
I'M *NOT* A PROFESSOR! AND DARK? ⇒PFF!⇐ I'M NOT AFRAID OF THE DARK!
UHHH...
ACTUALLY, JACK, WHY DON'T YOU GO ON AND SCOUT AHEAD OF US AND WE'LL BRING UP THE REAR?

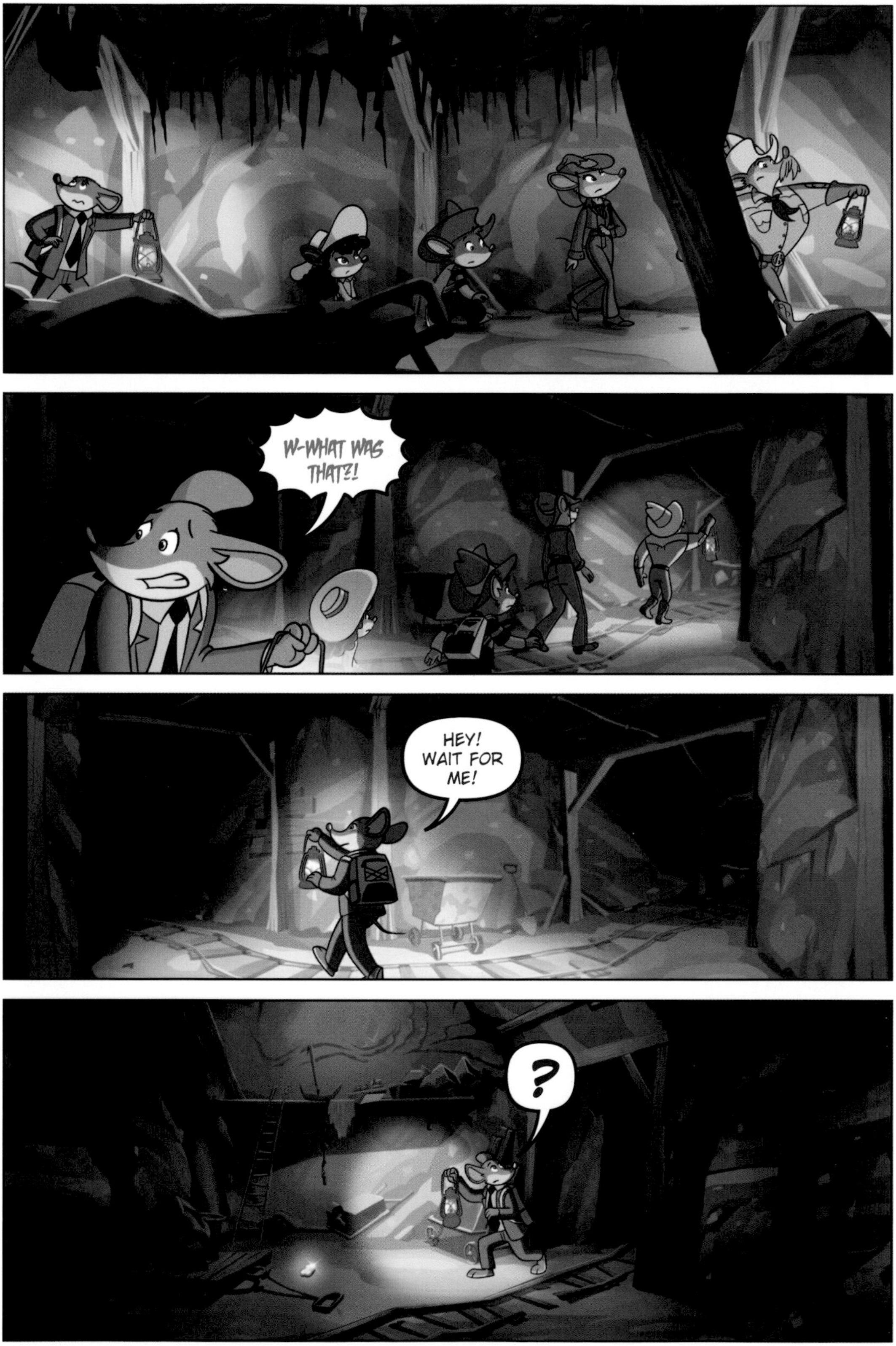
W-WHAT WAS THAT?!
HEY! WAIT FOR ME!
?

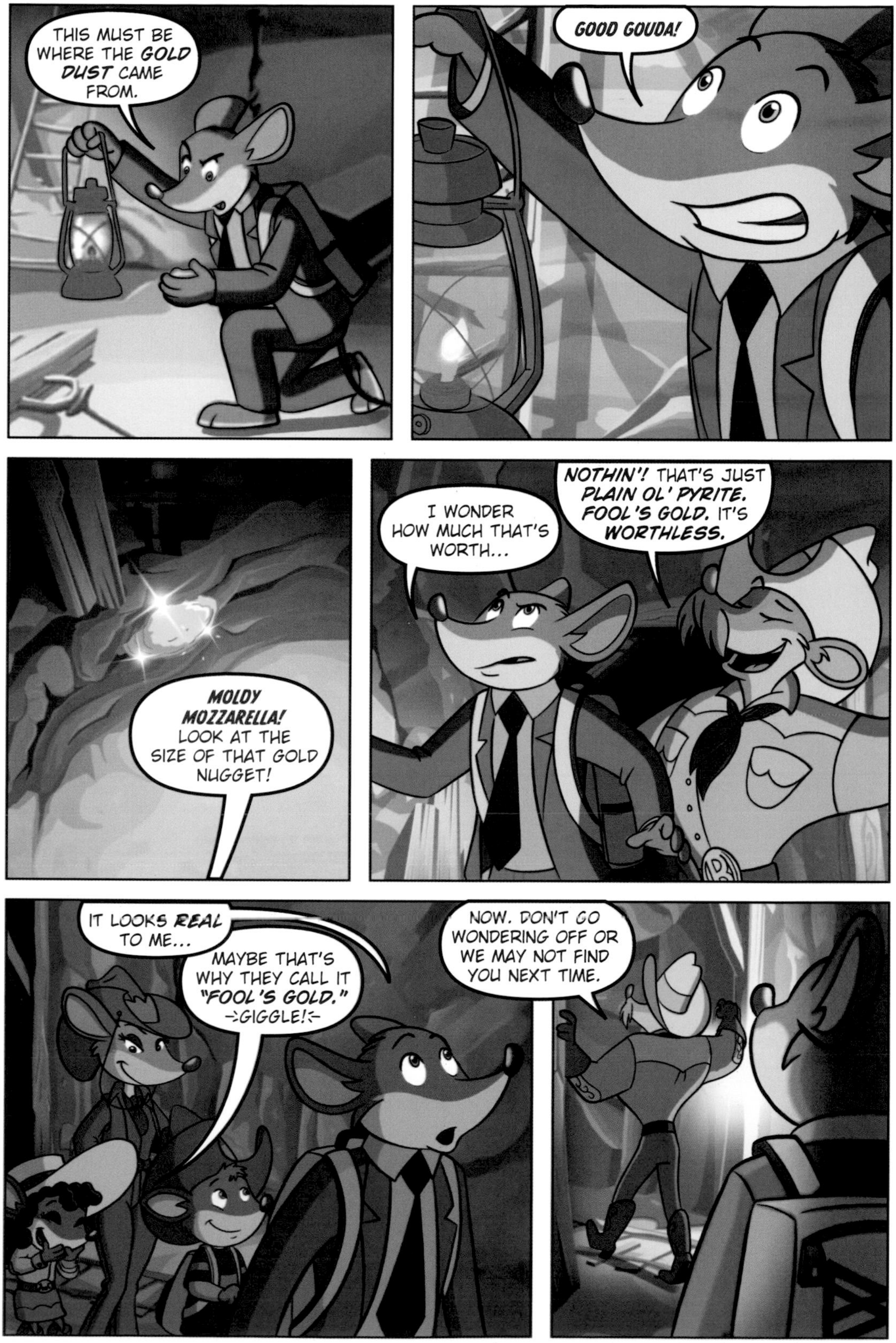
THIS MUST BE WHERE THE GOLD DUST CAME FROM.
GOOD GOUDA!
MOLDY MOZZARELLA! LOOK AT THE SIZE OF THAT GOLD NUGGET!
I WONDER HOW MUCH THAT'S WORTH...
NOTHIN'! THAT'S JUST PLAIN OL' PYRITE. FOOL'S GOLD. IT'S WORTHLESS.
IT LOOKS REAL TO ME...
MAYBE THAT'S WHY THEY CALL IT "FOOL'S GOLD." -GIGGLE!-
NOW. DON'T GO WONDERING OFF OR WE MAY NOT FIND YOU NEXT TIME.

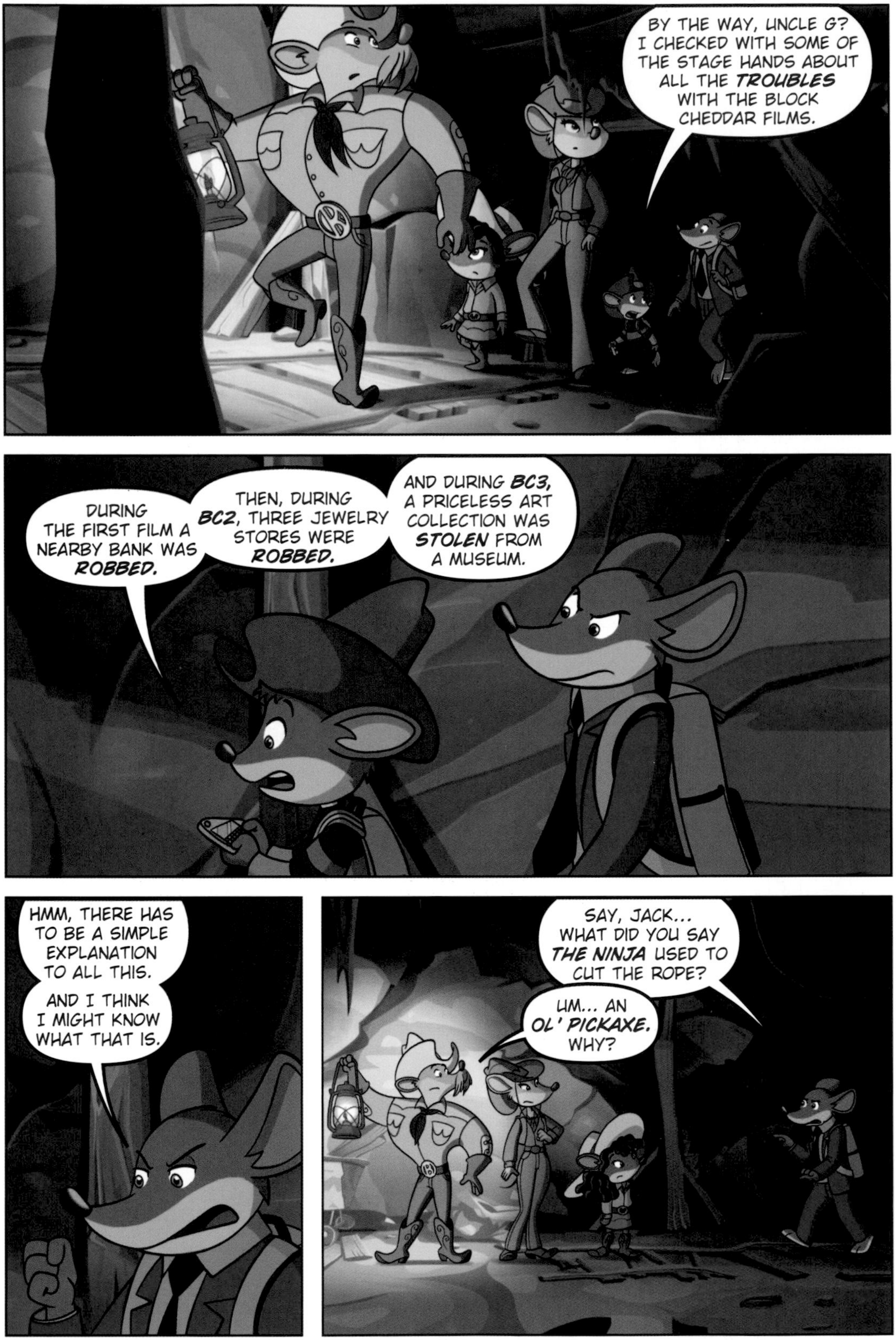

BY THE WAY, UNCLE G? I CHECKED WITH SOME OF THE STAGE HANDS ABOUT ALL THE **TROUBLES** WITH THE BLOCK CHEDDAR FILMS.
DURING THE FIRST FILM A NEARBY BANK WAS **ROBBED.**
THEN, DURING **BC2**, THREE JEWELRY STORES WERE **ROBBED.**
AND DURING **BC3,** A PRICELESS ART COLLECTION WAS **STOLEN** FROM A MUSEUM.
HMM, THERE HAS TO BE A SIMPLE EXPLANATION TO ALL THIS.
AND I THINK I MIGHT KNOW WHAT THAT IS.
SAY, JACK... WHAT DID YOU SAY **THE NINJA** USED TO CUT THE ROPE?
UM... AN **OL' PICKAXE.** WHY?

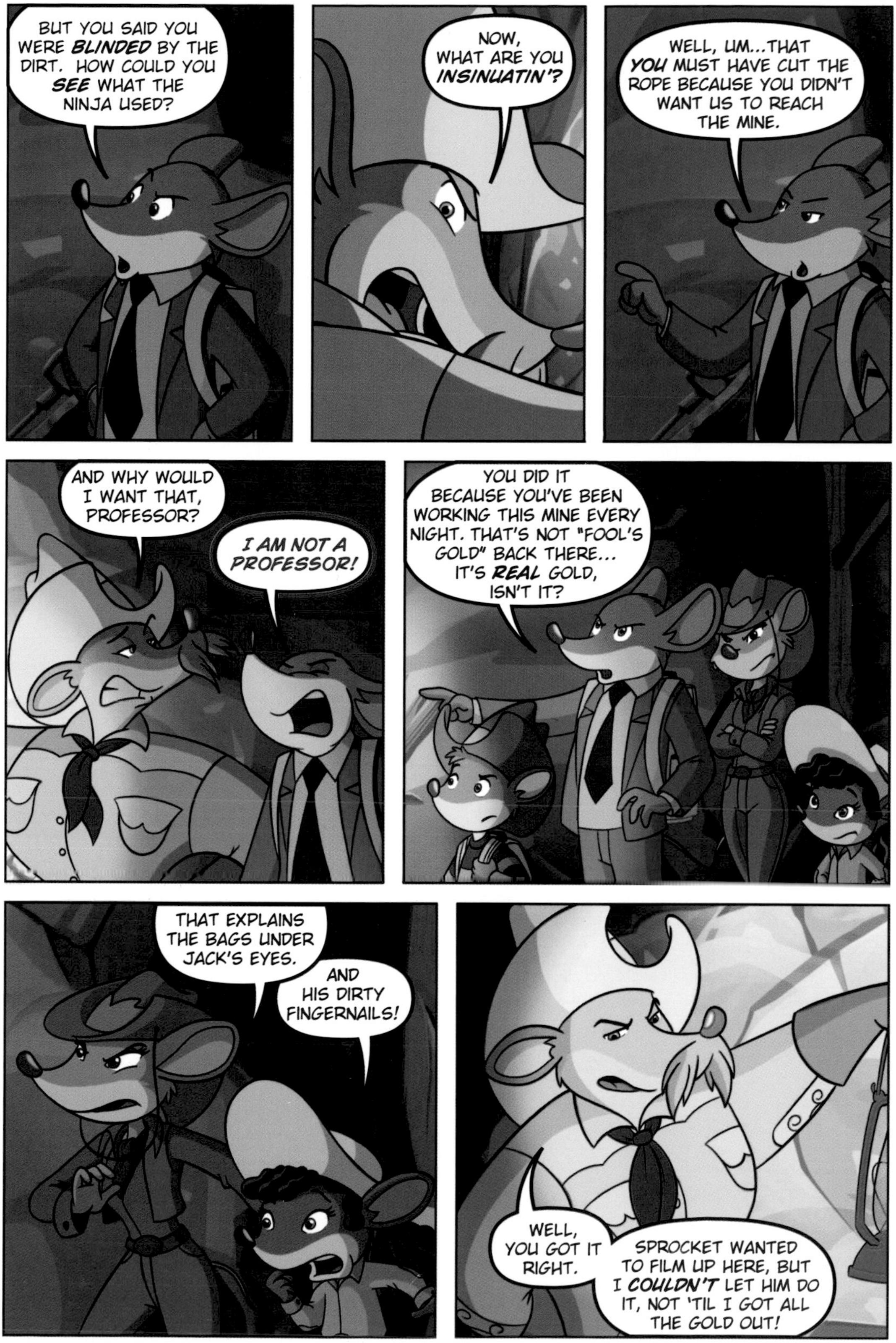
BUT YOU SAID YOU WERE BLINDED BY THE DIRT. HOW COULD YOU SEE WHAT THE NINJA USED?
NOW, WHAT ARE YOU INSINUATIN'?
WELL, UM...THAT YOU MUST HAVE CUT THE ROPE BECAUSE YOU DIDN'T WANT US TO REACH THE MINE.
AND WHY WOULD I WANT THAT, PROFESSOR?
I AM NOT A PROFESSOR!
YOU DID IT BECAUSE YOU'VE BEEN WORKING THIS MINE EVERY NIGHT. THAT'S NOT "FOOL'S GOLD" BACK THERE... IT'S REAL GOLD, ISN'T IT?
THAT EXPLAINS THE BAGS UNDER JACK'S EYES.
AND HIS DIRTY FINGERNAILS!
WELL, YOU GOT IT RIGHT.
SPROCKET WANTED TO FILM UP HERE, BUT I COULDN'T LET HIM DO IT, NOT 'TIL I GOT ALL THE GOLD OUT!

WELL, I'D LIKE TO JAW SOME MORE, BUT I GOTTA GET *GOIN'*.

Y'ALL, ON THE OTHER HAND, GOTTA STAY HERE...*FOR GOOD!*

AAAAH!

FSSST

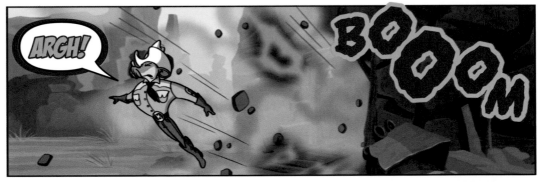

ARGH!

BOOOM

THAT OUGHTA KEEP THEM OUT OF MY BUSINESS.

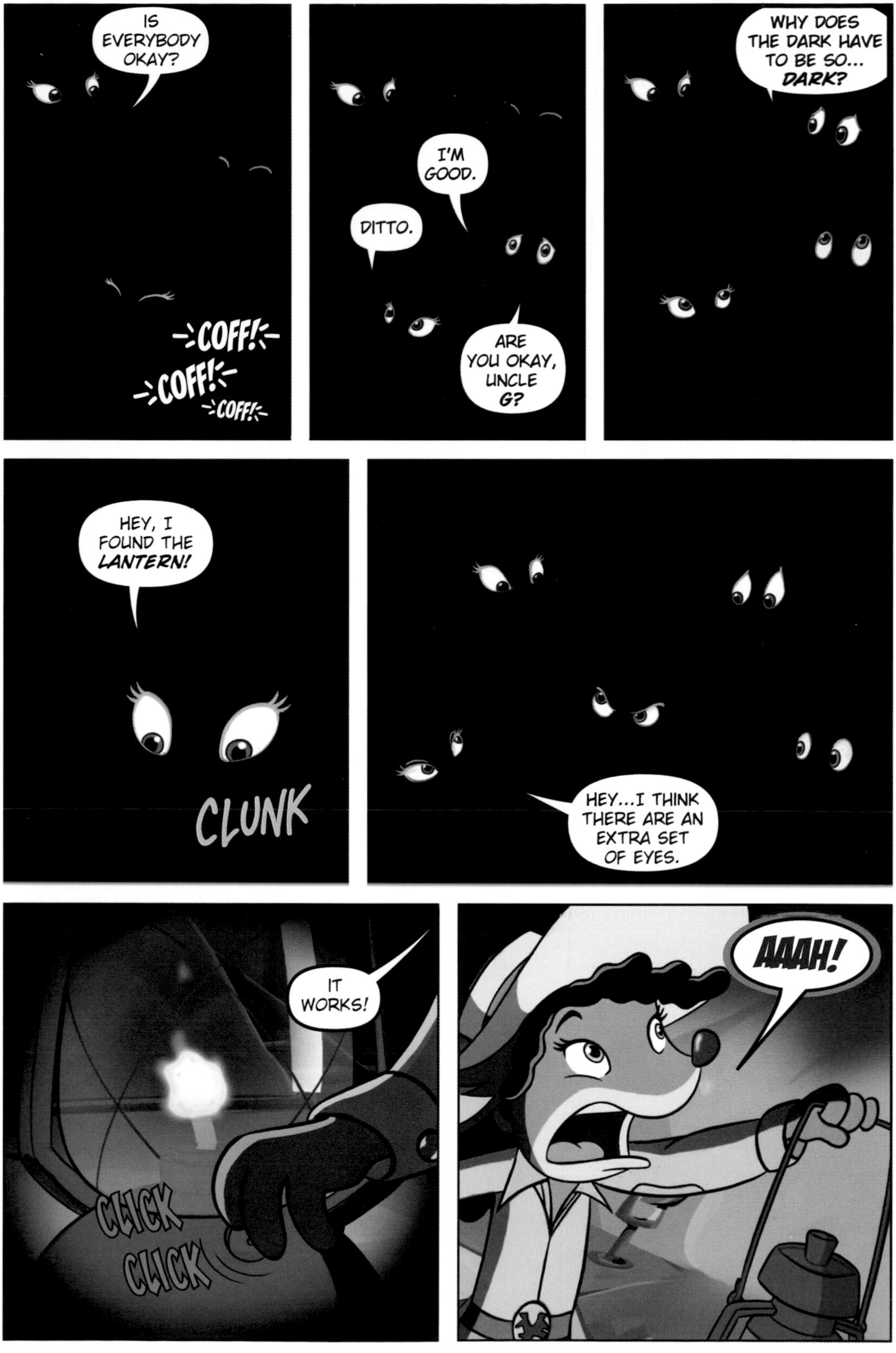
IS EVERYBODY OKAY?
COFF! COFF! COFF!
I'M GOOD.
DITTO.
ARE YOU OKAY, UNCLE G?
WHY DOES THE DARK HAVE TO BE SO... DARK?
HEY, I FOUND THE LANTERN!
CLUNK
HEY...I THINK THERE ARE AN EXTRA SET OF EYES.
IT WORKS!
CLICK CLICK
AAAH!

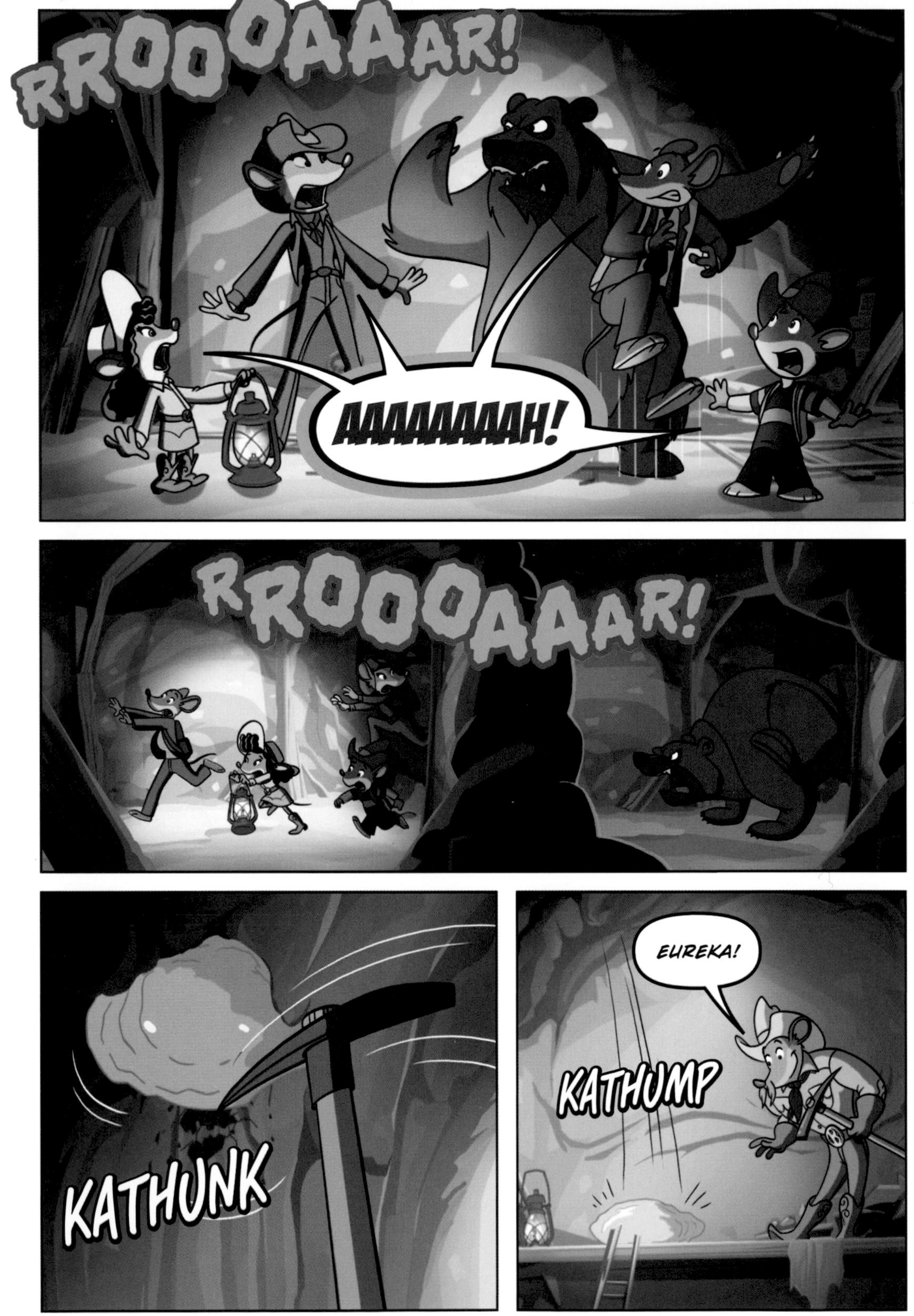
RROOOAAAR!
AAAAAAAAH!
RROOOAAAR!
KATHUNK
EUREKA!
KATHUMP

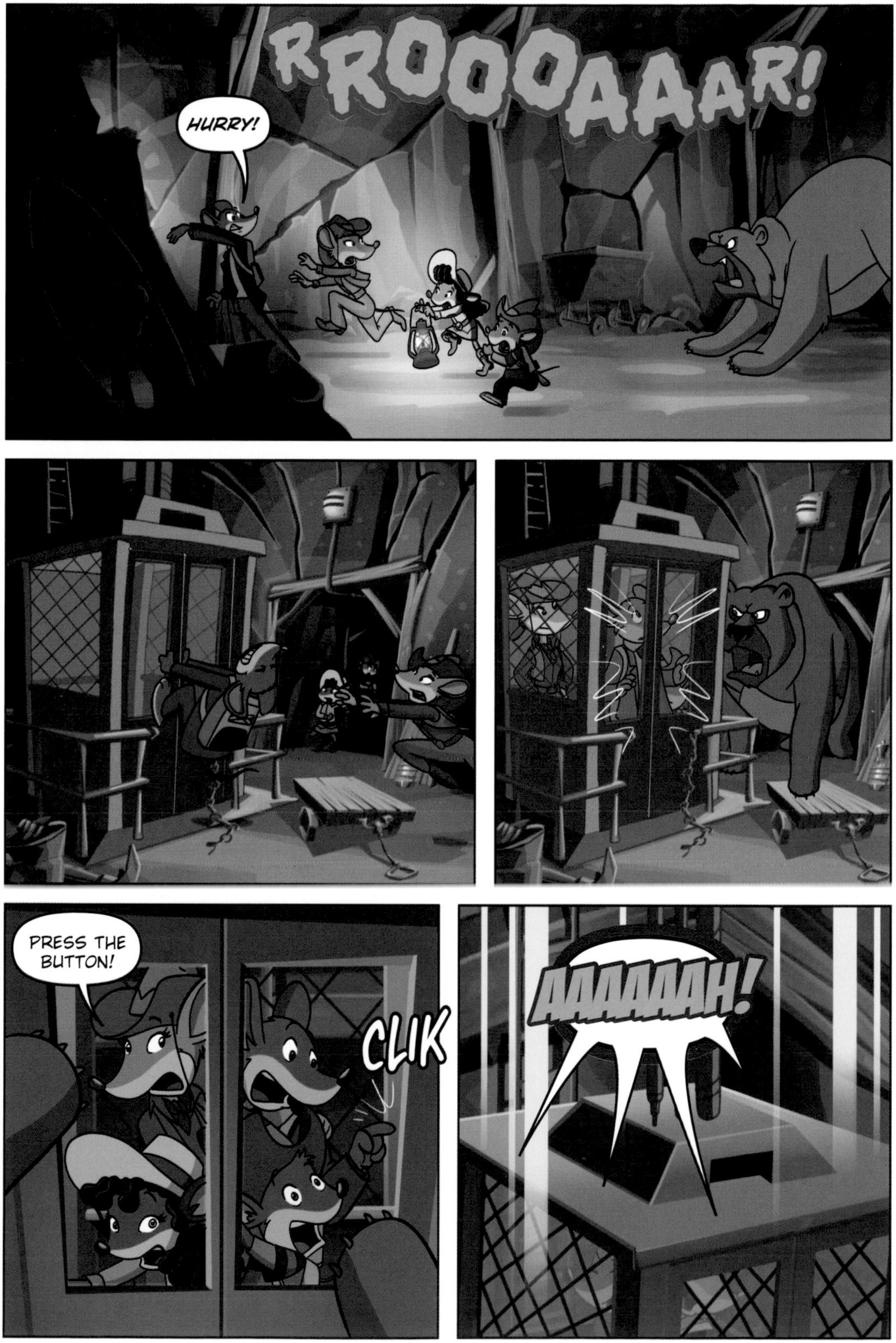
RROOOAAAR!
HURRY!
PRESS THE BUTTON!
CLIK
AAAAAAH!

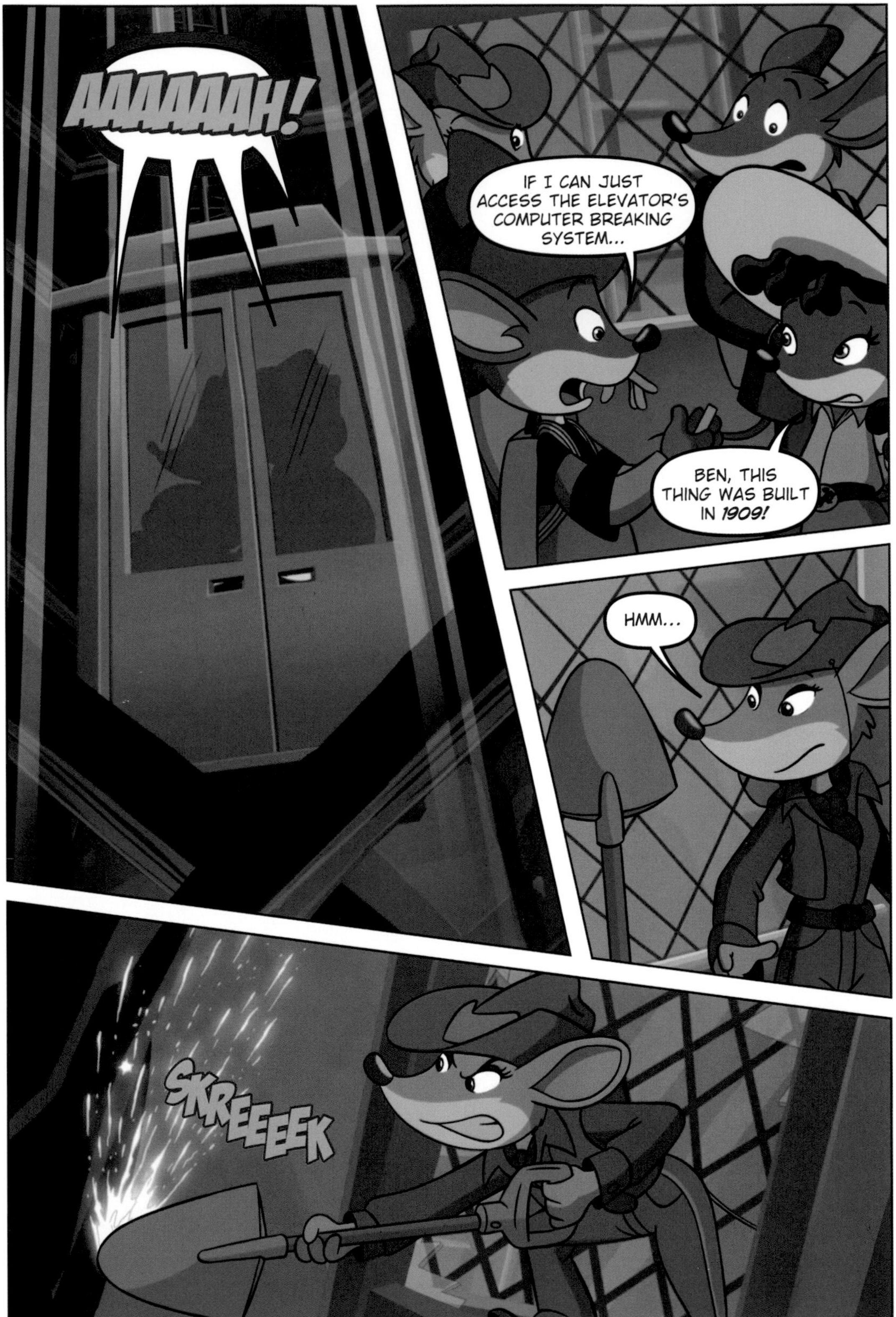
AAAAAAH!
IF I CAN JUST ACCESS THE ELEVATOR'S COMPUTER BREAKING SYSTEM...
BEN, THIS THING WAS BUILT IN *1909!*
HMM...
SKREEEEK

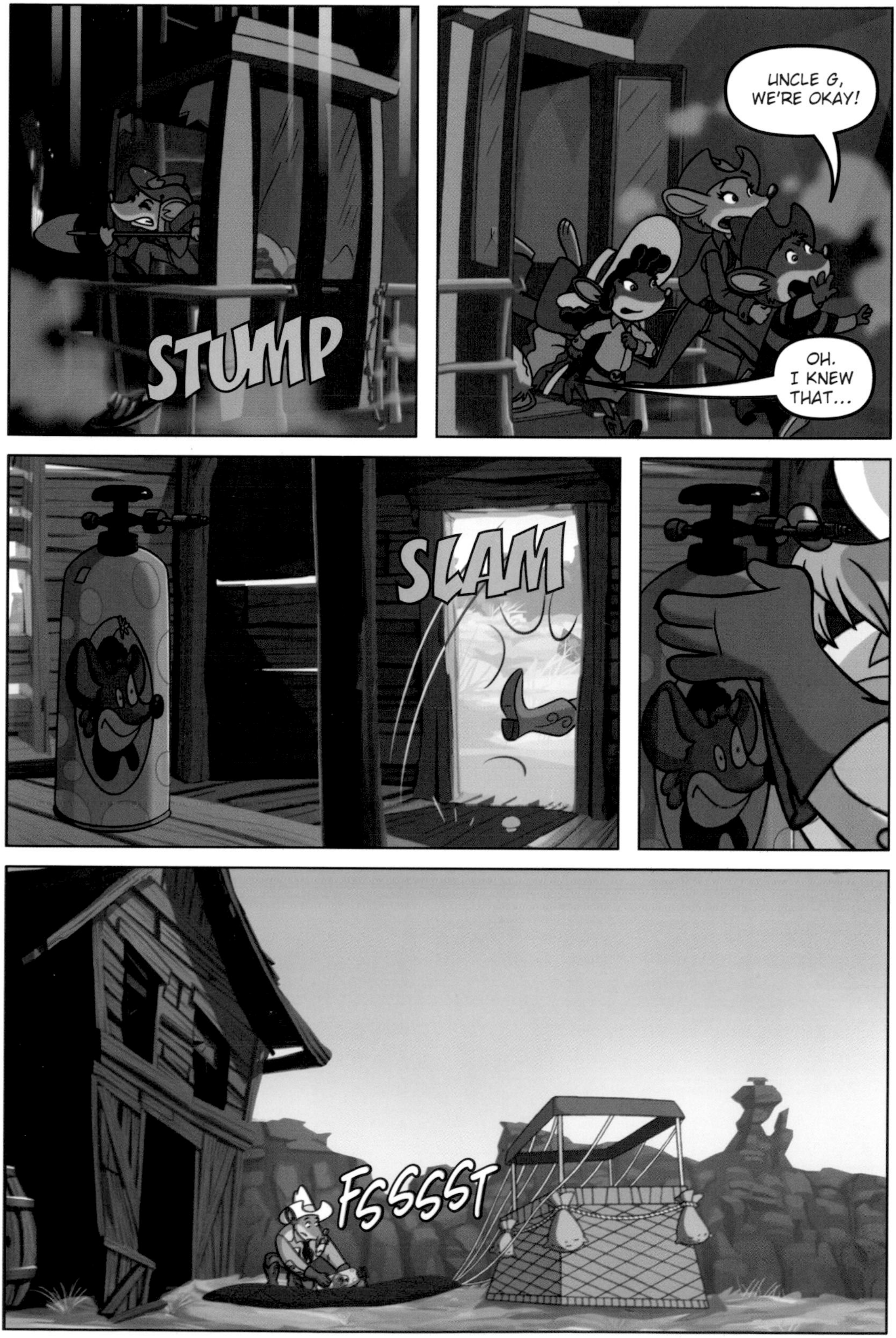
STUMP
UNCLE G, WE'RE OKAY!
OH. I KNEW THAT...
SLAM
FSSSST

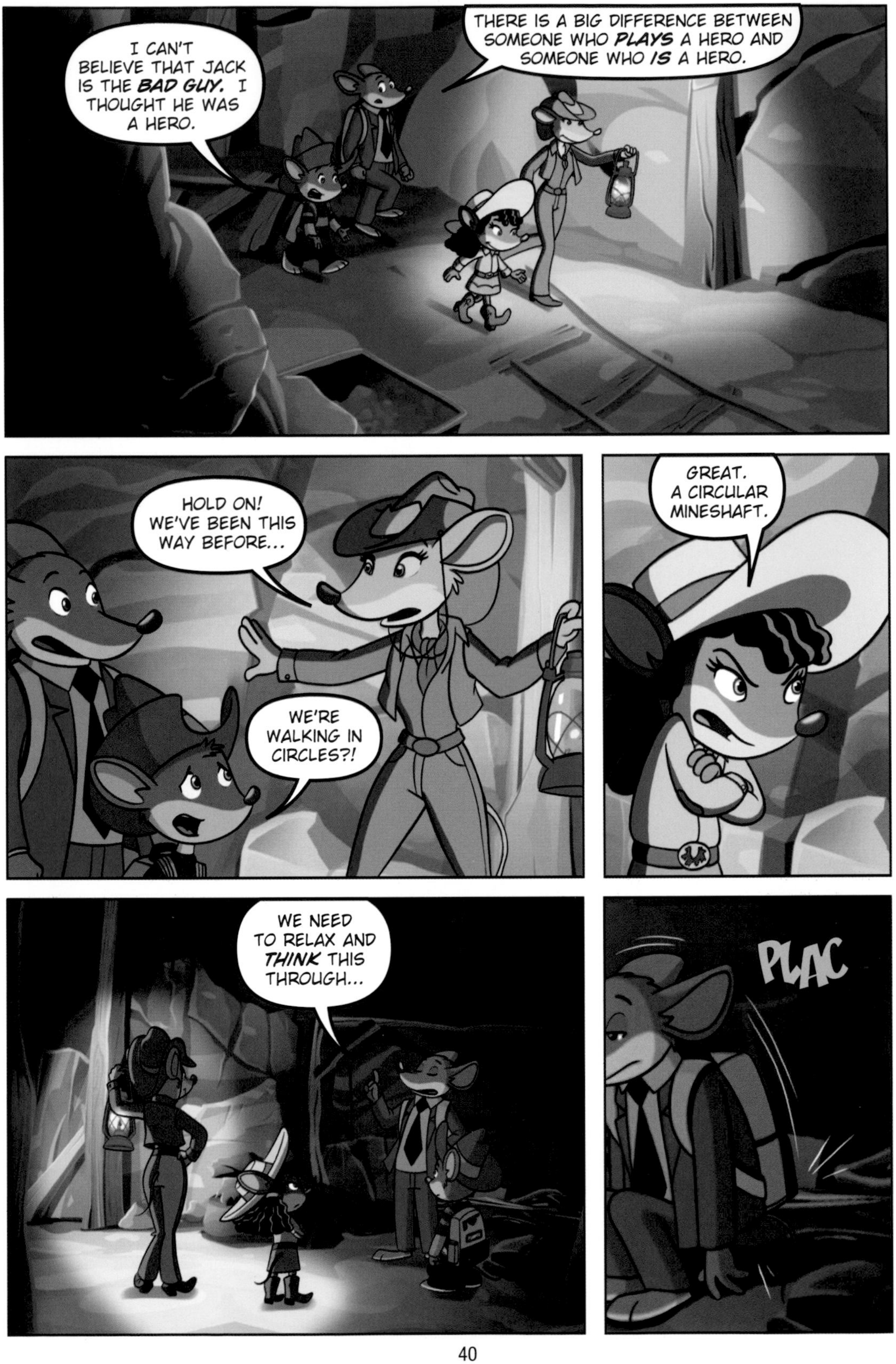

I CAN'T BELIEVE THAT JACK IS THE ***BAD GUY.*** I THOUGHT HE WAS A HERO.
THERE IS A BIG DIFFERENCE BETWEEN SOMEONE WHO ***PLAYS*** A HERO AND SOMEONE WHO ***IS*** A HERO.
HOLD ON! WE'VE BEEN THIS WAY BEFORE...
WE'RE WALKING IN CIRCLES?!
GREAT. A CIRCULAR MINESHAFT.
WE NEED TO RELAX AND ***THINK*** THIS THROUGH...
PLAC

RrRuuUMBLE

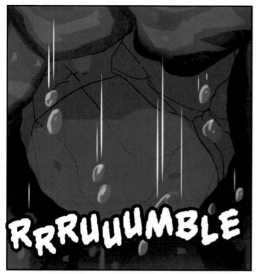

SKraKt

WBram

RrRuuUMBLE

RUN!

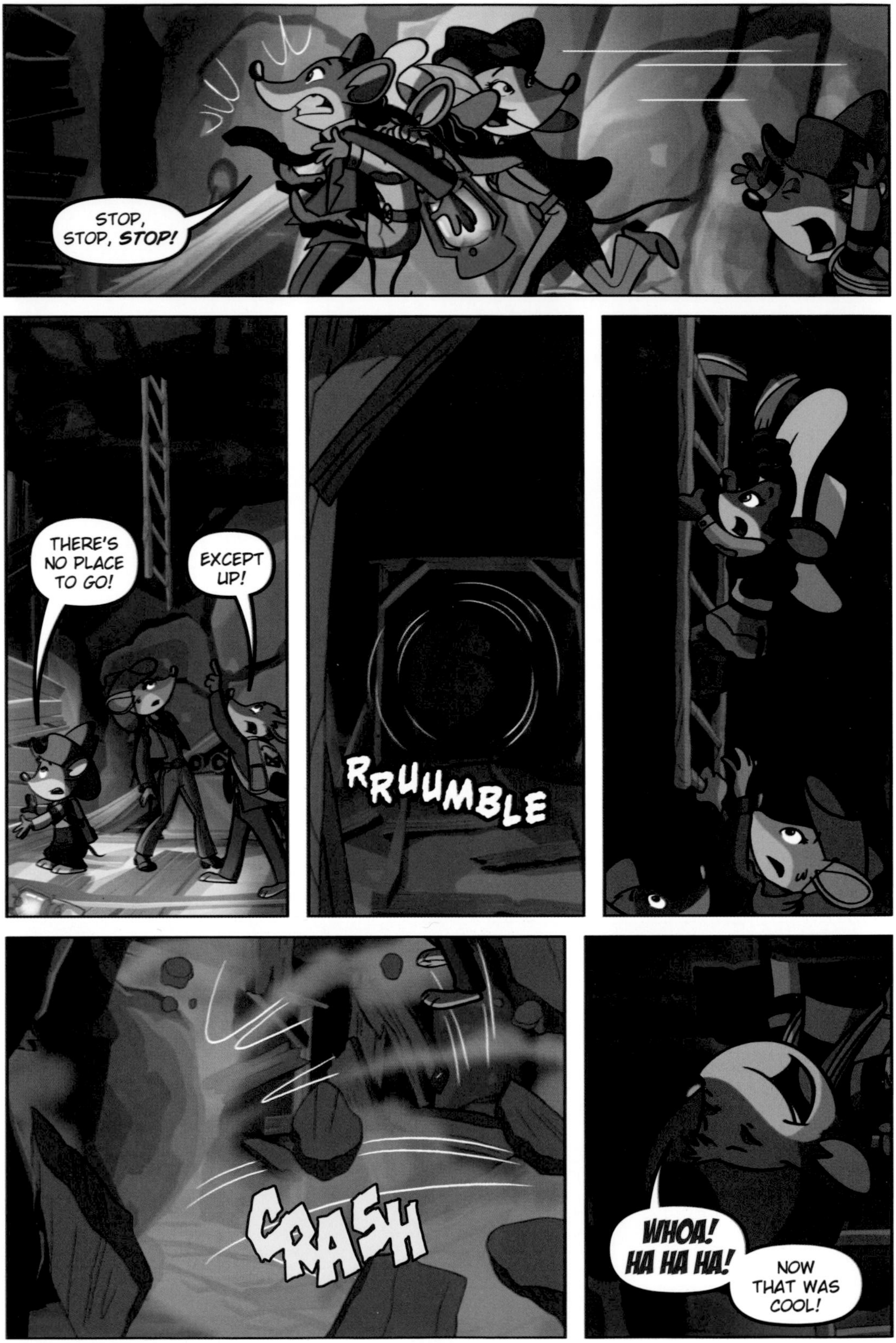
STOP, STOP, STOP!
THERE'S NO PLACE TO GO!
EXCEPT UP!
RRUUMBLE
CRASH
WHOA! HA HA HA!
NOW THAT WAS COOL!

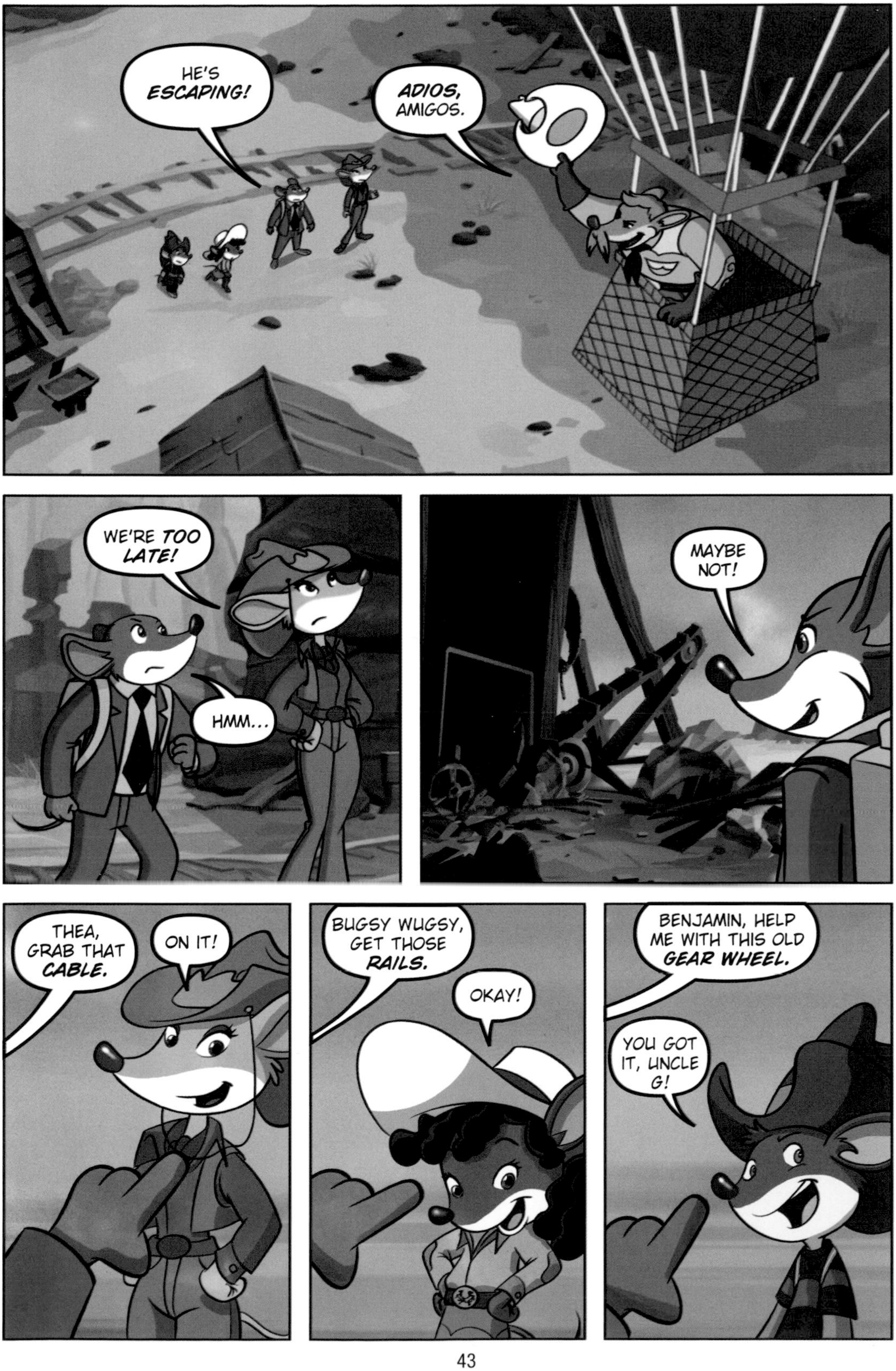
HE'S ESCAPING!
ADIOS, AMIGOS.
WE'RE TOO LATE!
HMM...
MAYBE NOT!
THEA, GRAB THAT CABLE.
ON IT!
BUGSY WUGSY, GET THOSE RAILS.
OKAY!
BENJAMIN, HELP ME WITH THIS OLD GEAR WHEEL.
YOU GOT IT, UNCLE G!

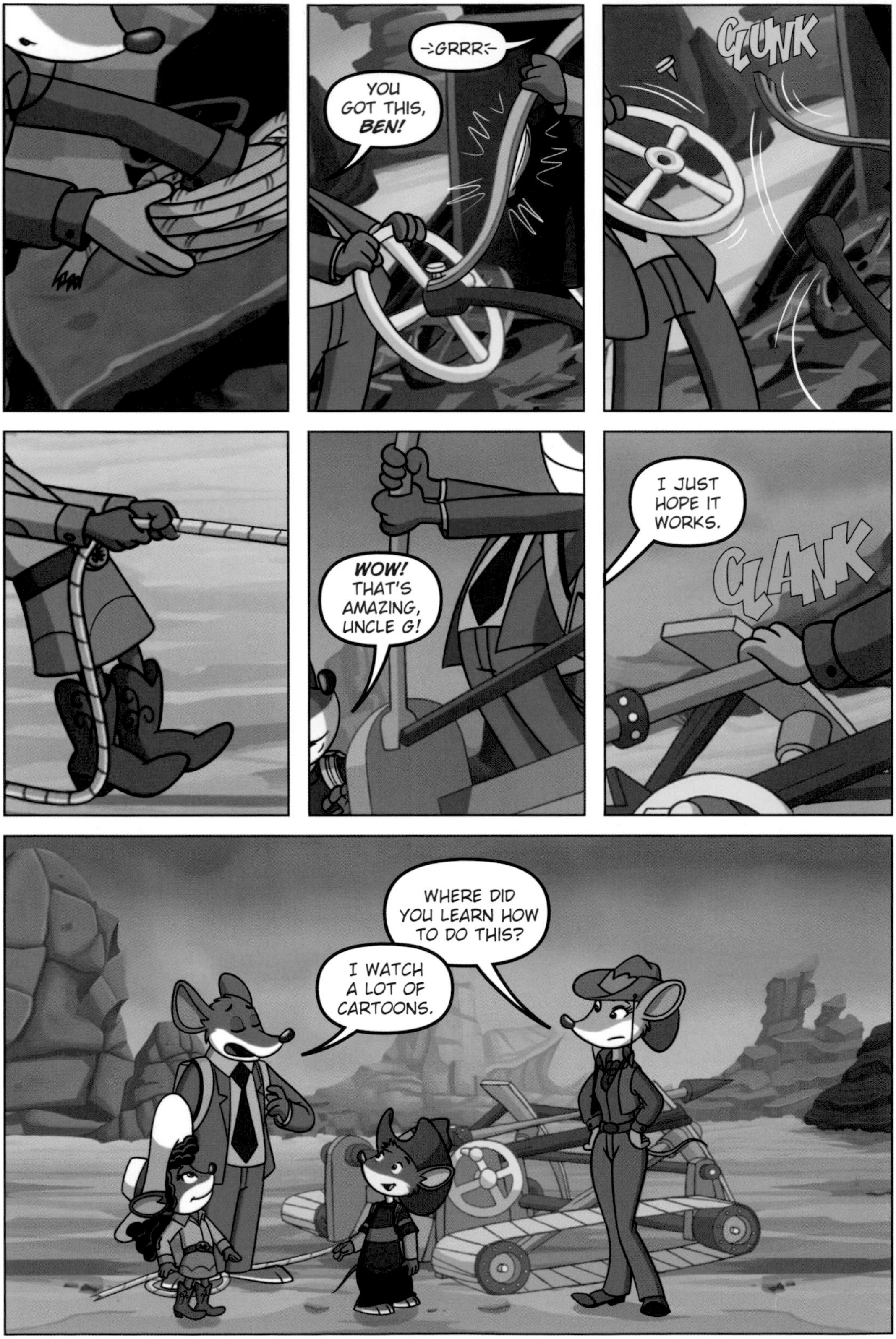

-GRRR-
YOU GOT THIS, BEN!
CLUNK
WOW! THAT'S AMAZING, UNCLE G!
I JUST HOPE IT WORKS.
CLANK
WHERE DID YOU LEARN HOW TO DO THIS?
I WATCH A LOT OF CARTOONS.

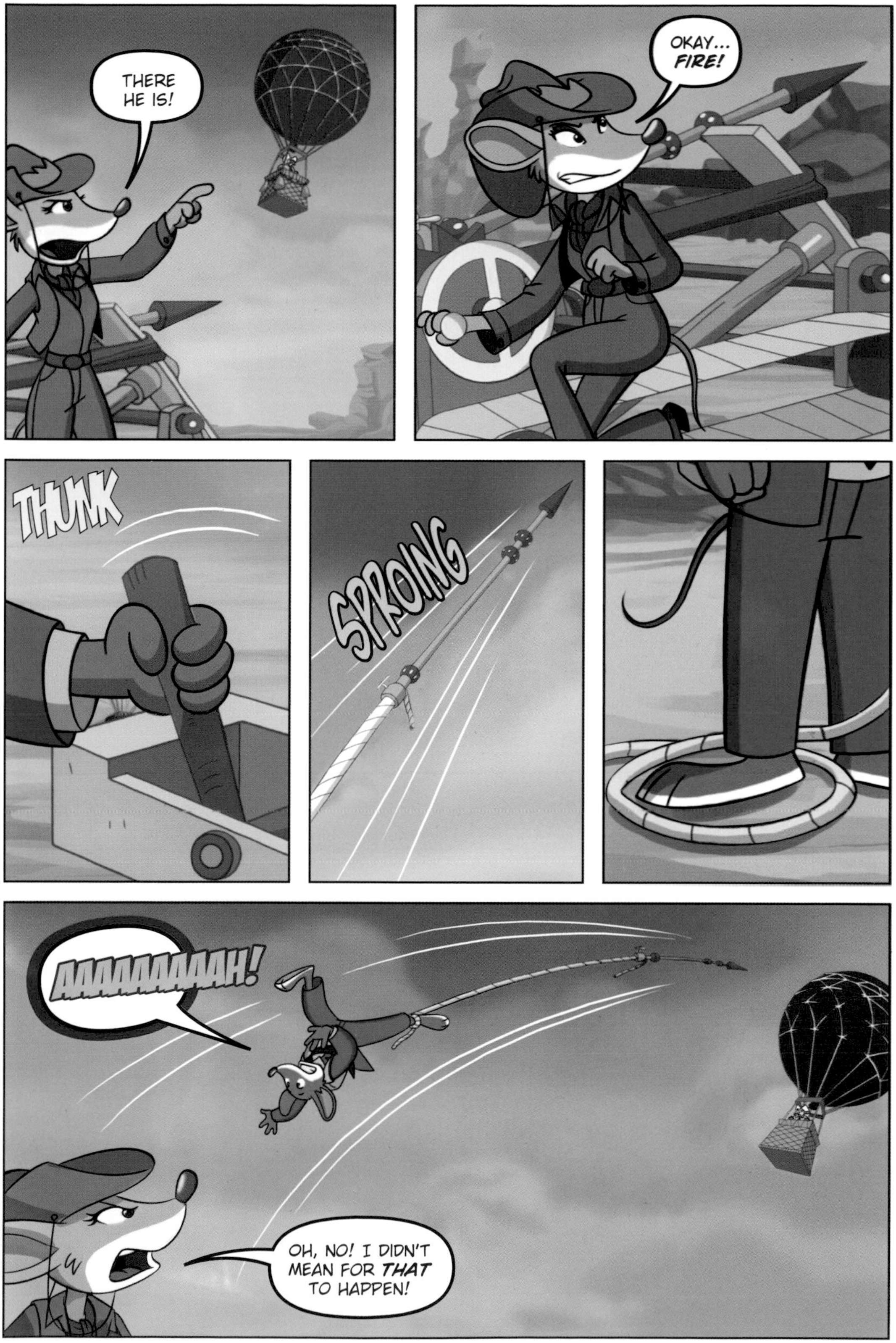
THERE HE IS!
OKAY... *FIRE!*
THUNK
SPROING
AAAAAAAAAH!
OH, NO! I DIDN'T MEAN FOR *THAT* TO HAPPEN!

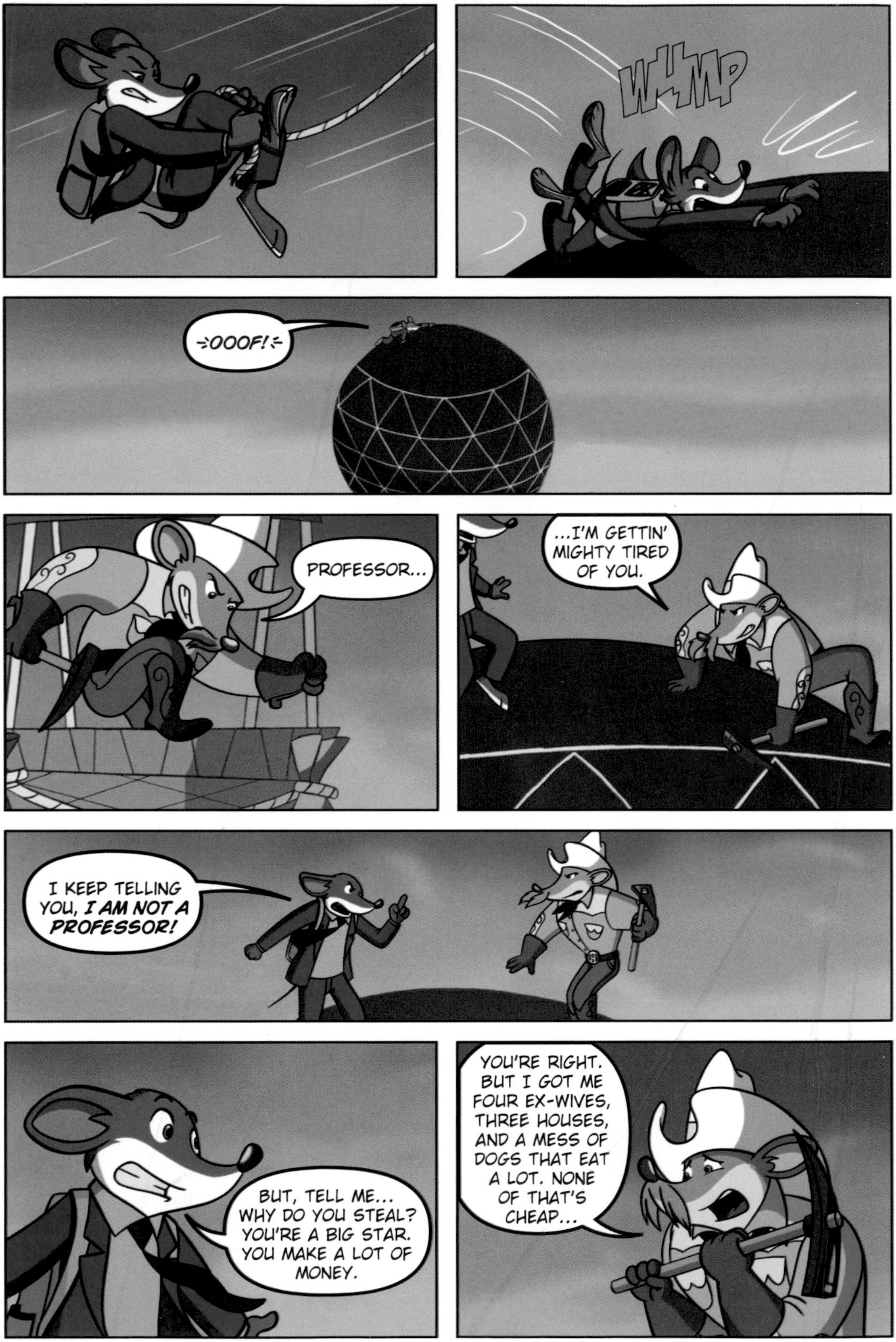
WHUMP
OOOF!
PROFESSOR...
...I'M GETTIN' MIGHTY TIRED OF YOU.
I KEEP TELLING YOU, *I AM NOT A PROFESSOR!*
BUT, TELL ME... WHY DO YOU STEAL? YOU'RE A BIG STAR. YOU MAKE A LOT OF MONEY.
YOU'RE RIGHT. BUT I GOT ME FOUR EX-WIVES, THREE HOUSES, AND A MESS OF DOGS THAT EAT A LOT. NONE OF THAT'S CHEAP...

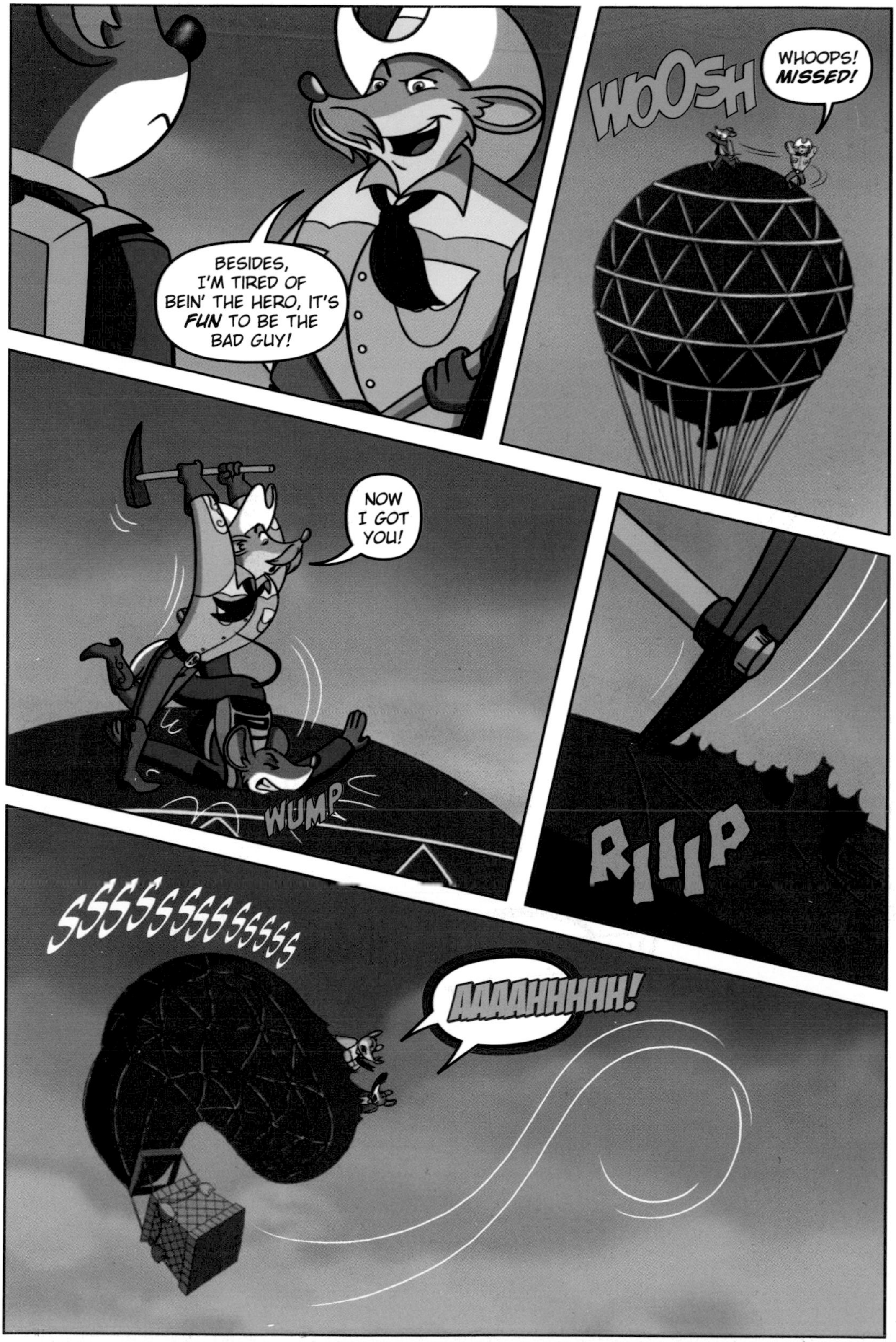

BESIDES, I'M TIRED OF BEIN' THE HERO, IT'S FUN TO BE THE BAD GUY!
WOOSH
WHOOPS! MISSED!
NOW I GOT YOU!
WUMP
RIIIP
SSSSSSSSSSSSSS
AAAAHHHHH!

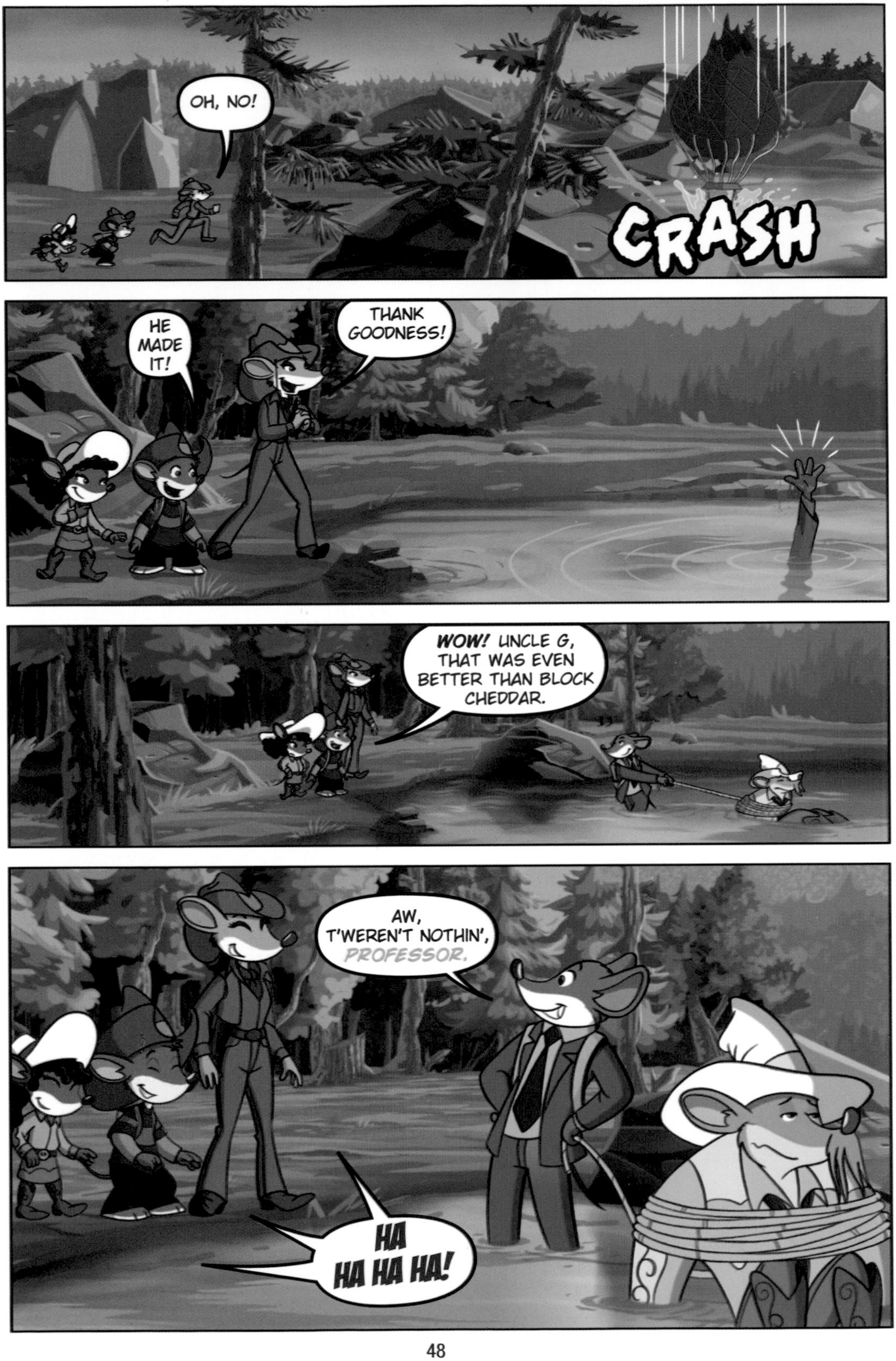
OH, NO!
CRASH
HE MADE IT!
THANK GOODNESS!
WOW! UNCLE G, THAT WAS EVEN BETTER THAN BLOCK CHEDDAR.
AW, T'WEREN'T NOTHIN', PROFESSOR.
HA HA HA HA!

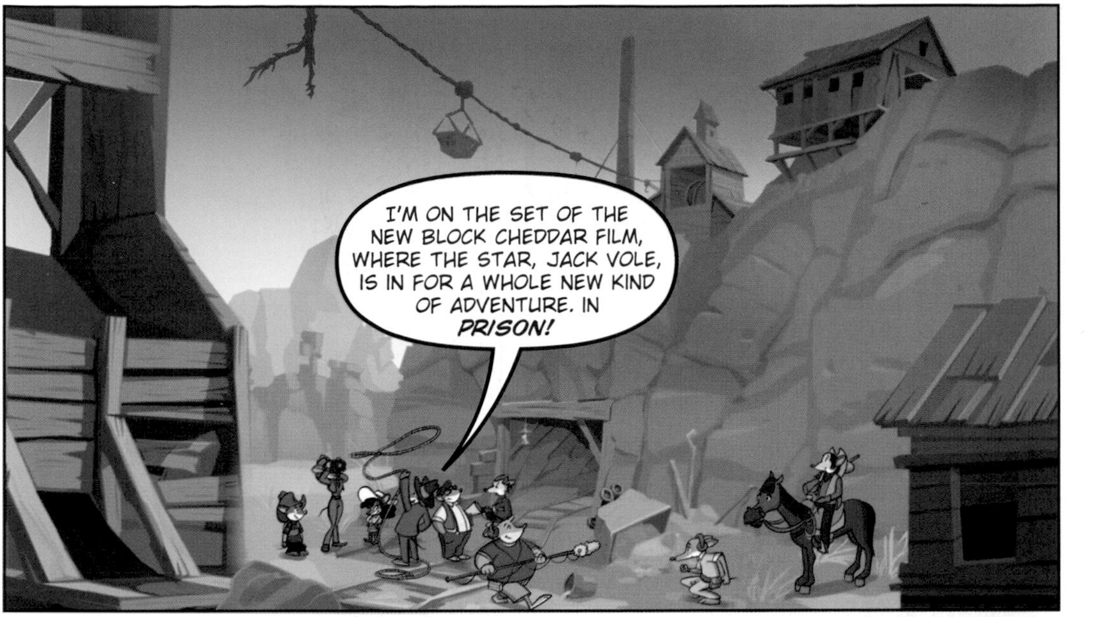
I'M ON THE SET OF THE NEW BLOCK CHEDDAR FILM, WHERE THE STAR, JACK VOLE, IS IN FOR A WHOLE NEW KIND OF ADVENTURE. IN PRISON!
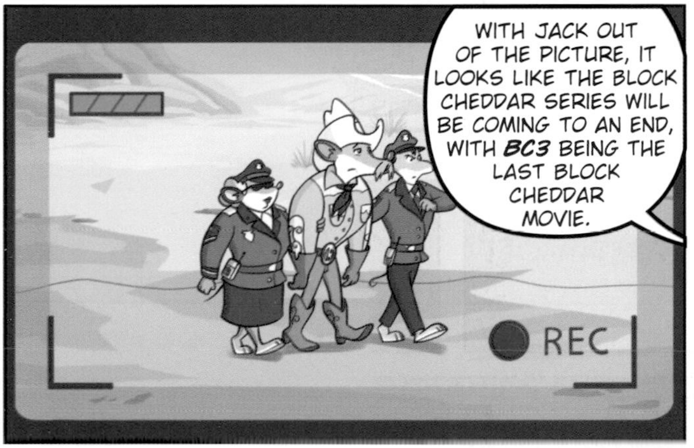
WITH JACK OUT OF THE PICTURE, IT LOOKS LIKE THE BLOCK CHEDDAR SERIES WILL BE COMING TO AN END, WITH BC3 BEING THE LAST BLOCK CHEDDAR MOVIE.
REC
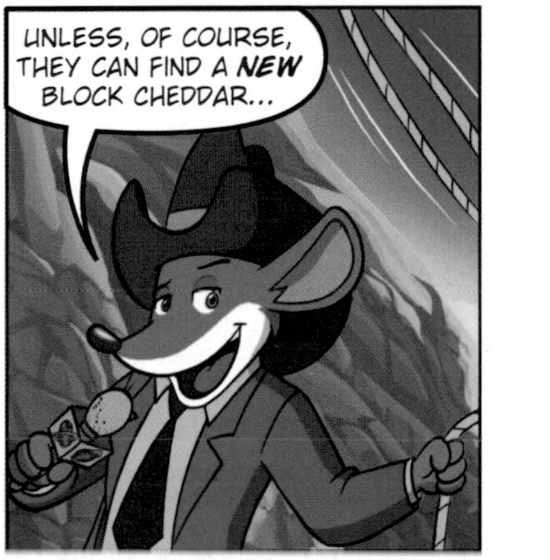
UNLESS, OF COURSE, THEY CAN FIND A NEW BLOCK CHEDDAR...
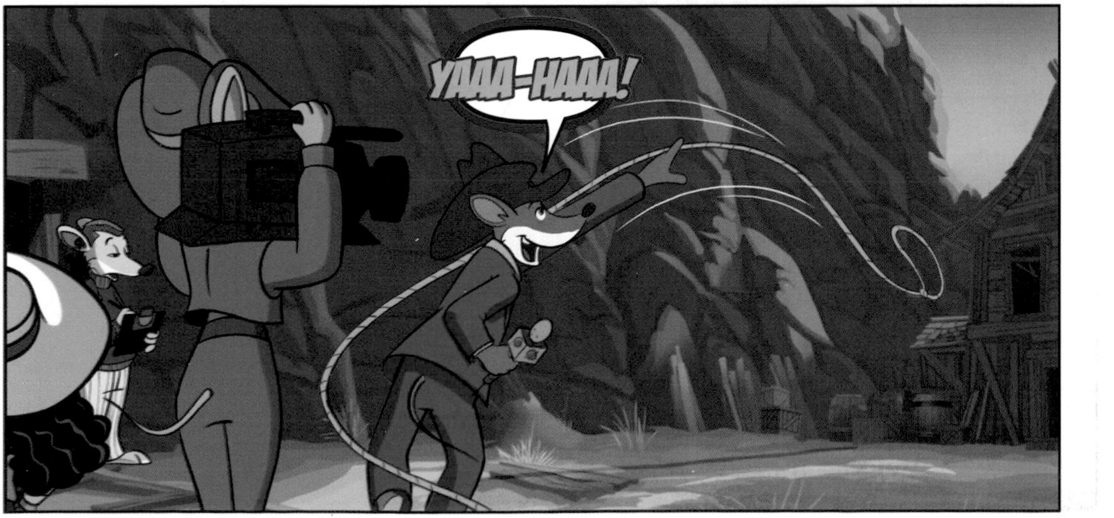
YAAA-HAAA!

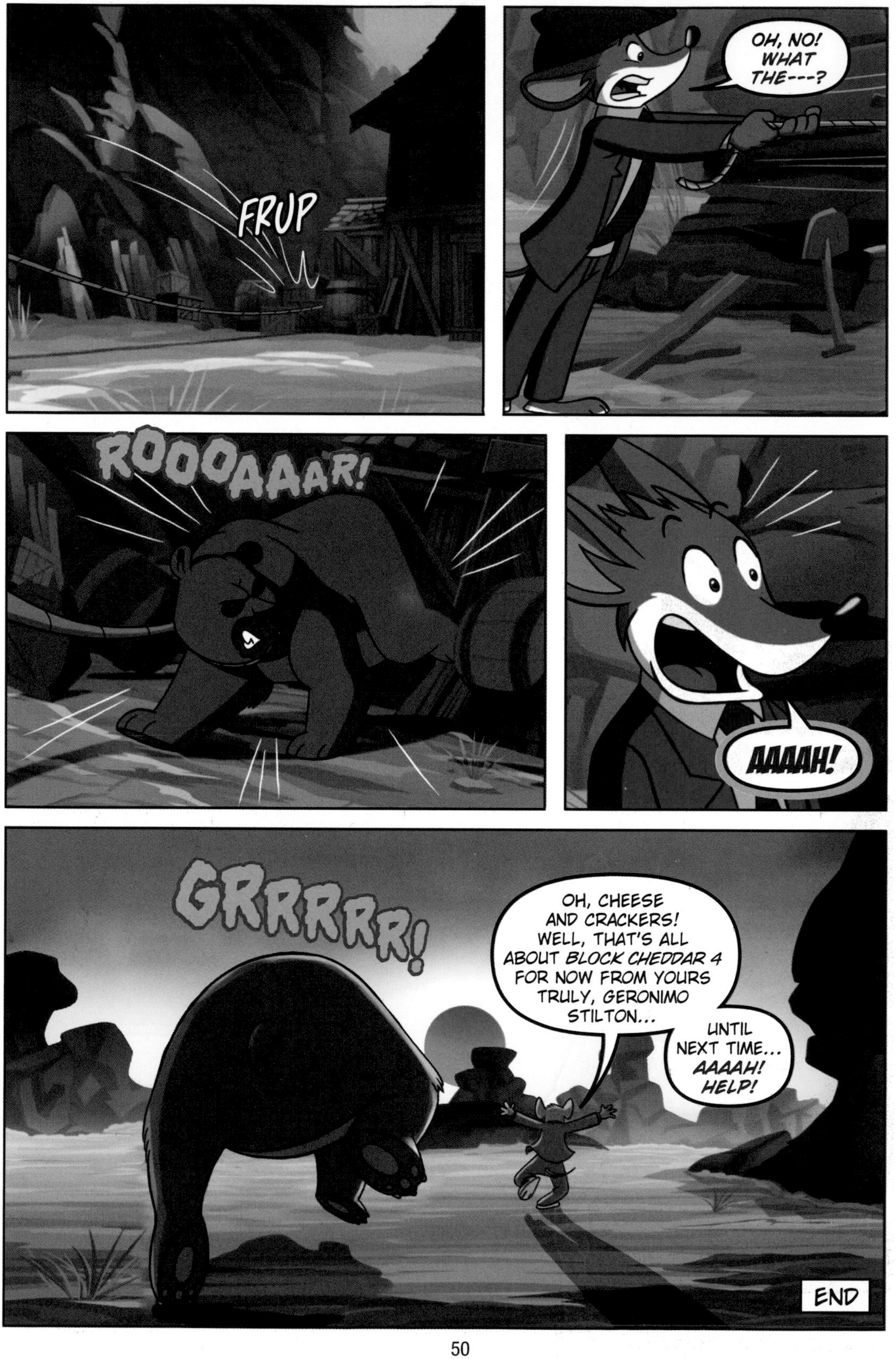
FRUP
OH, NO! WHAT THE---?
ROOOAAAR!
AAAAH!
GRRRRRR!
OH, CHEESE AND CRACKERS! WELL, THAT'S ALL ABOUT *BLOCK CHEDDAR 4* FOR NOW FROM YOURS TRULY, GERONIMO STILTON...
UNTIL NEXT TIME... *AAAAH! HELP!*
END

Watch Out For PAPERCUT Z™

Welcome to the trail-blazing, tumbleweed-kicking, third GERONIMO STILTON REPORTER graphic novel, "Stop Acting Around," the official comics adaptation of the third episode of Geronimo Stilton Season One, written by Rob Humphrey and John Behnke, brought to you by Papercutz — those tenderfoots and city-slickers dedicated to publishing great graphic novels for all ages. I'm Salicrup, *Jim Salicrup,* the Editor-in-Chief and Geronimo's stunt double.

Before we go any further, let's make sure we all understand which GERONIMO STILTON series is which. It all began with the long-running series of GERONIMO STILTON chapter books from our friends at Scholastic. Papercutz (that's us) then joined in with a series of GERONIMO STILTON graphic novels, that featured Geronimo's adventures saving the future, by protecting the past, usually from those pesky Pirate Cats. That time-traveling series ran for nineteen volumes, which are now being collected in GERONIMO STILTON 3 IN 1, which collects three graphic novels in each specially priced volume. Then there's this all-new series, GERONIMO STILTON REPORTER, which brings you the official comics adaptations of the animated Geronimo Stilton TV series, seen on Netflix and Amazon Prime. Papercutz also publishes eight volumes of THEA STILTON, which features the Thea Sisters – Colette, Nicky, Pamela, Paulina, and Violet – five fun, lively students at Mouseford Academy on Whale Island, who want to be real live journalists like their hero, Thea Stilton.

As you can see, Geronimo Stilton sure gets around! But despite appearing in so many chapter books, graphic novels, and animated TV shows, there are certain core values that are always present in each and every Geronimo Stilton story. You can find those values described in great detail on geronimostilton.com in a section called The Philosophy of Geronimo Stilton. We've also been talking about those values, in the *Watch Out for Papercutz* pages in GERONIMO STILTON 3 IN 1, and here in GERONIMO STILTON REPORTER. This time, we'd like to talk about…

GERONIMO STILTON AND WORK
Geronimo loves his job and always says: "Oh, how I love books! I like reading them, flicking through them; I love the smell of fresh ink on freshly printed pages! How wonderful it is to be a publisher!"
Geronimo works a lot and is always busy. But he does it with joy, because working is his life and he feels privileged to be able to do a job that he likes so much.
Geronimo approaches his work in a deeply ethical way: he puts his heart into every story that he writes, to inspire courage, optimism, and energy.
A book written from the heart is different from others. It's more beautiful, more real, better!

No wonder I identify so strongly with Geronimo Stilton, as editor-in-chief of Papercutz, I feel exactly the same way as he does! I too love books. I too like reading them, flicking through them, and I even love the smell of fresh ink on freshly printed Papercutz graphic novels! That doesn't mean I don't enjoy digital versions of books and comics – I do! – but I'm a bit of a dinosaur like Geronimo and simply love printed books, magazines, and comics. It's probably a generational thing – when I was growing up, there simply weren't any digital books of any kind!

Also, just like Geronimo, I love my job! I've been fortunate enough to be working in comics since I was 15 years-old, and I'm just as excited to be involved in creating comics today as I was back then. And like Geronimo, I put my heart into every Papercutz (and our wonderful imprints, Charmz and Super Genius) graphic novel we publish.

I consider myself incredibly lucky. I was lucky to figure out at an early age what I wanted to do with my life, and I was lucky to actually be able to do it! I can only wish that you too will be able to pursue your dreams, and get to live them. And don't worry if you're not sure yet what you want to do with the rest of your life. Don't put pressure on yourself to figure it out; you'll have plenty of time! What you can do in the meantime is prepare yourself both mentally and physically to be ready for whatever it might be. That's exactly what school is for.

And while we're all waiting to see what the future will bring, don't forget that GERONIMO STILTON REPORTER #4 "The Mummy with No Name," is coming soon to booksellers and libraries everywhere. Check out the special preview on the following pages. And don't miss Geronimo's animated adventures on Netflix and Amazon Prime! See you in the future!

Thanks again,

STAY IN TOUCH!

EMAIL:	salicrup@papercutz.com
WEB:	papercutz.com
TWITTER:	@papercutzgn
INSTAGRAM:	@papercutzgn
FACEBOOK:	PAPERCUTZGRAPHICNOVELS
SNAIL MAIL:	Papercutz, 160 Broadway, Suite 700, East Wing, New York, NY 10038

Special Preview of GERONIMO STILTON REPORTER Graphic Novel #4
"The Mummy with No Name"!

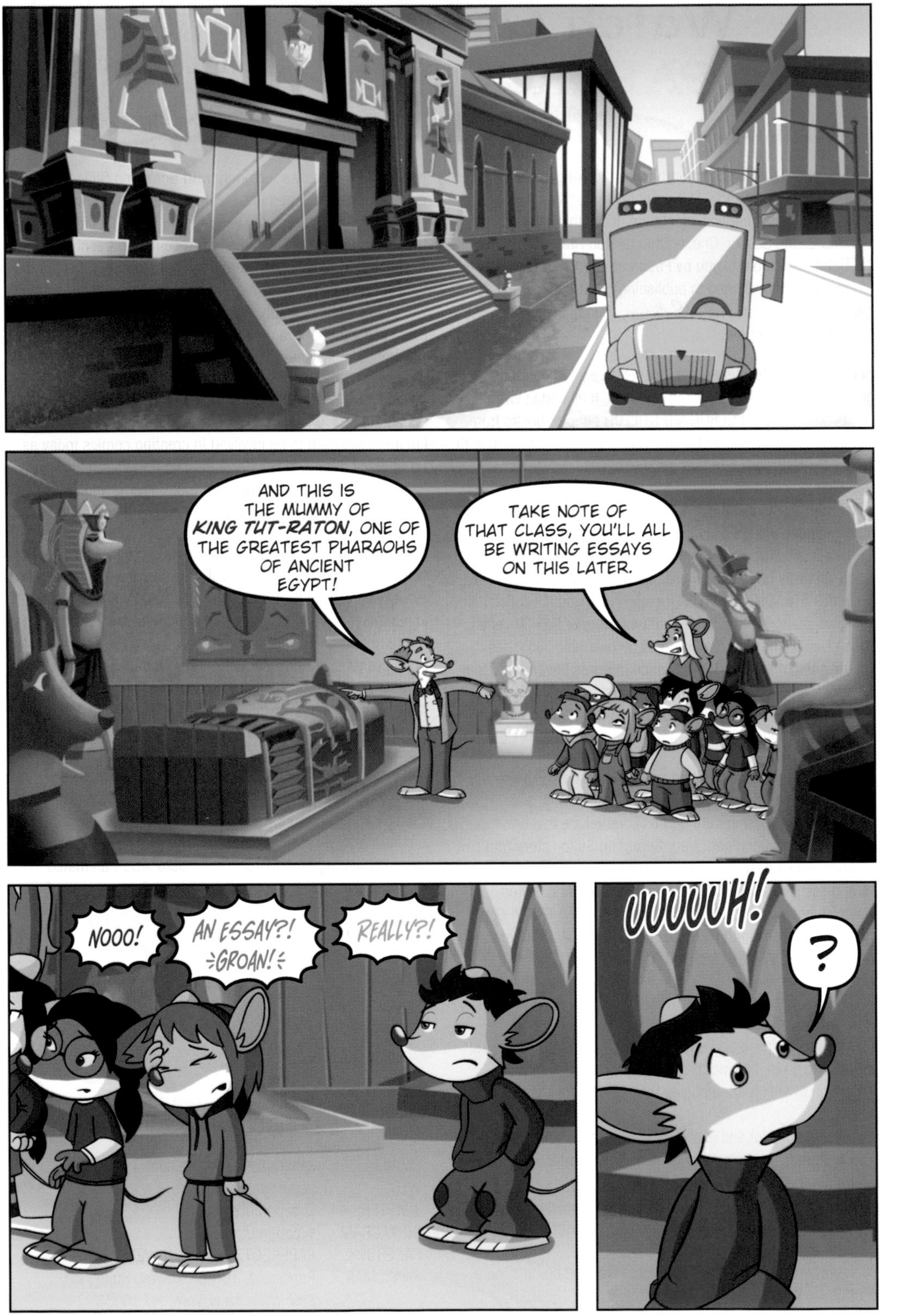
AND THIS IS THE MUMMY OF *KING TUT-RATON*, ONE OF THE GREATEST PHARAOHS OF ANCIENT EGYPT!
TAKE NOTE OF THAT CLASS, YOU'LL ALL BE WRITING ESSAYS ON THIS LATER.
NOOO!
AN ESSAY?! GROAN!
REALLY?!
UUUUUH!
?

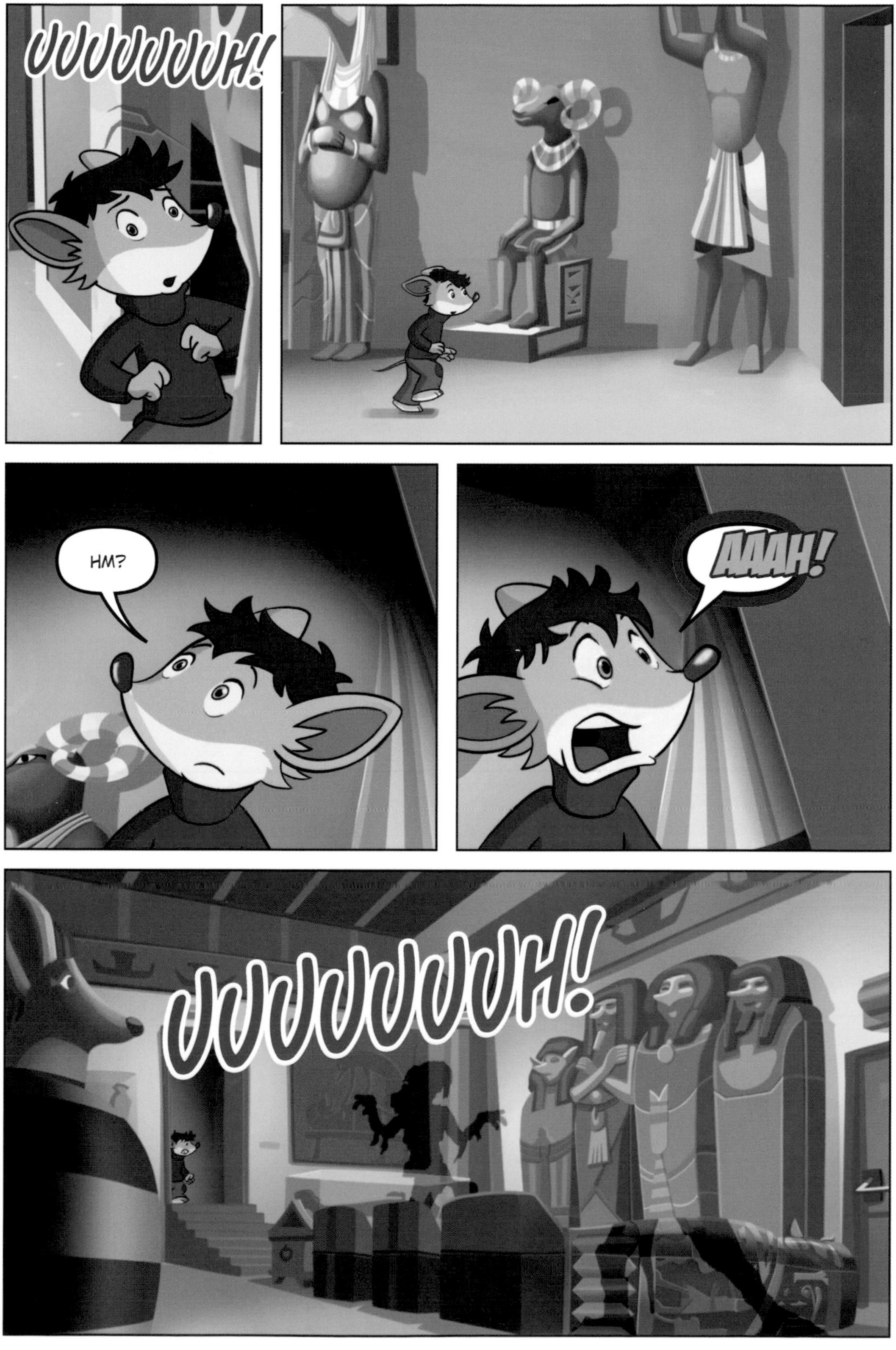
UUUUUUUUH!
HM?
AAAH!
UUUUUUUUUH!

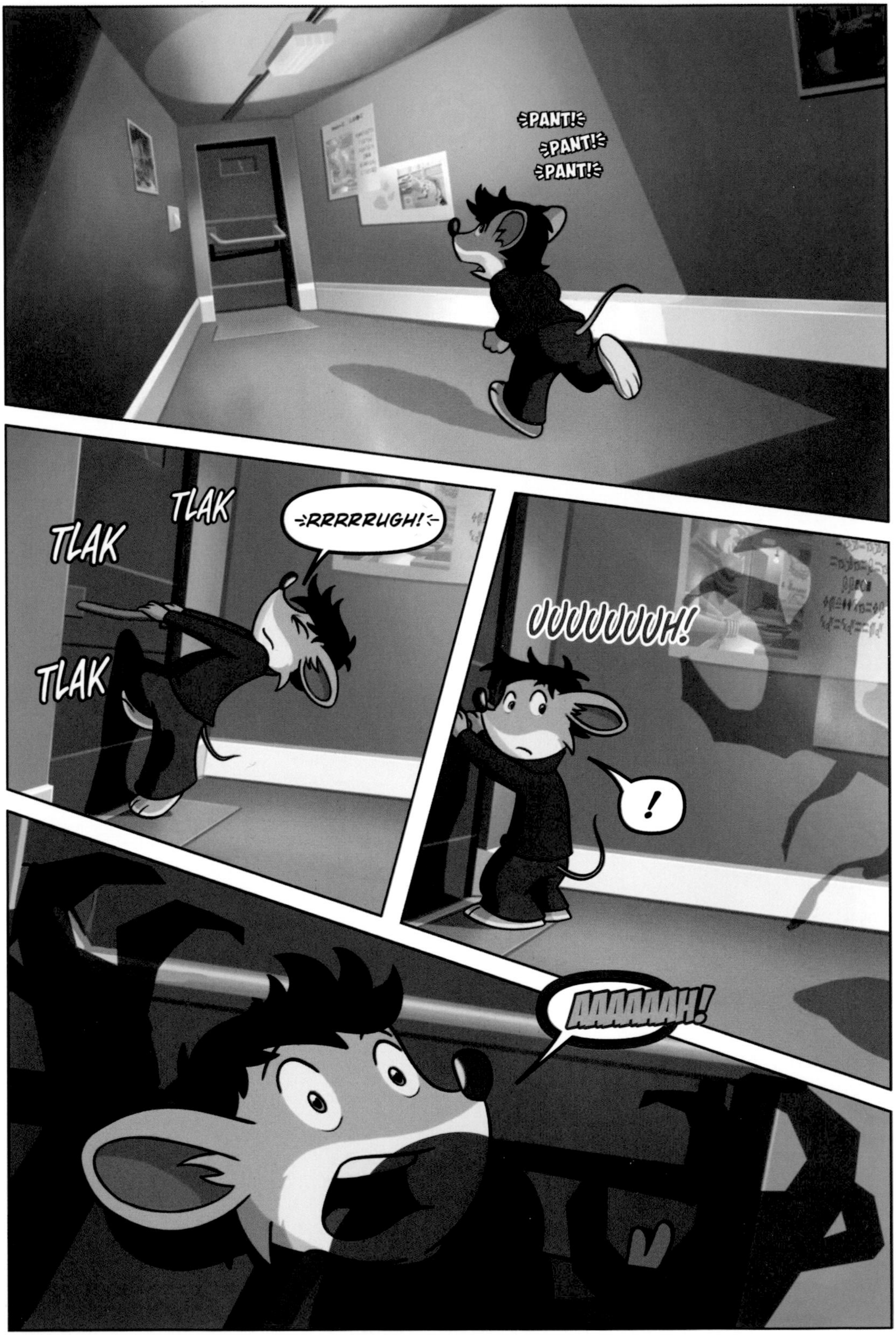
PANT!
PANT!
PANT!
TLAK
TLAK
TLAK
RRRRRUGH!
UUUUUUUH!
!
AAAAAAH!

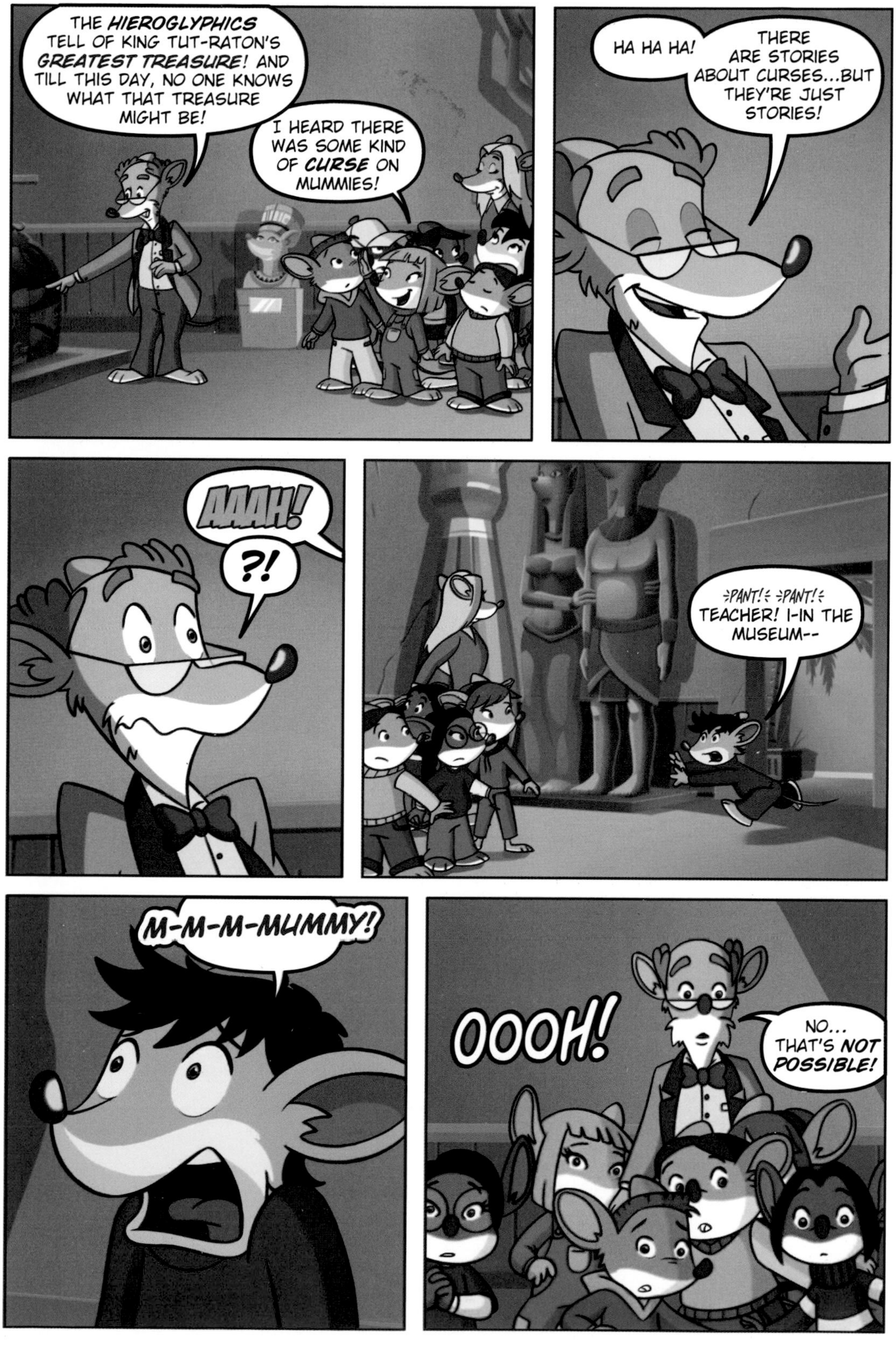
THE HIEROGLYPHICS TELL OF KING TUT-RATON'S GREATEST TREASURE! AND TILL THIS DAY, NO ONE KNOWS WHAT THAT TREASURE MIGHT BE!
I HEARD THERE WAS SOME KIND OF CURSE ON MUMMIES!
HA HA HA!
THERE ARE STORIES ABOUT CURSES...BUT THEY'RE JUST STORIES!
AAAH!
?!
PANT! PANT!
TEACHER! I-IN THE MUSEUM--
M-M-M-MUMMY!
OOOH!
NO... THAT'S NOT POSSIBLE!

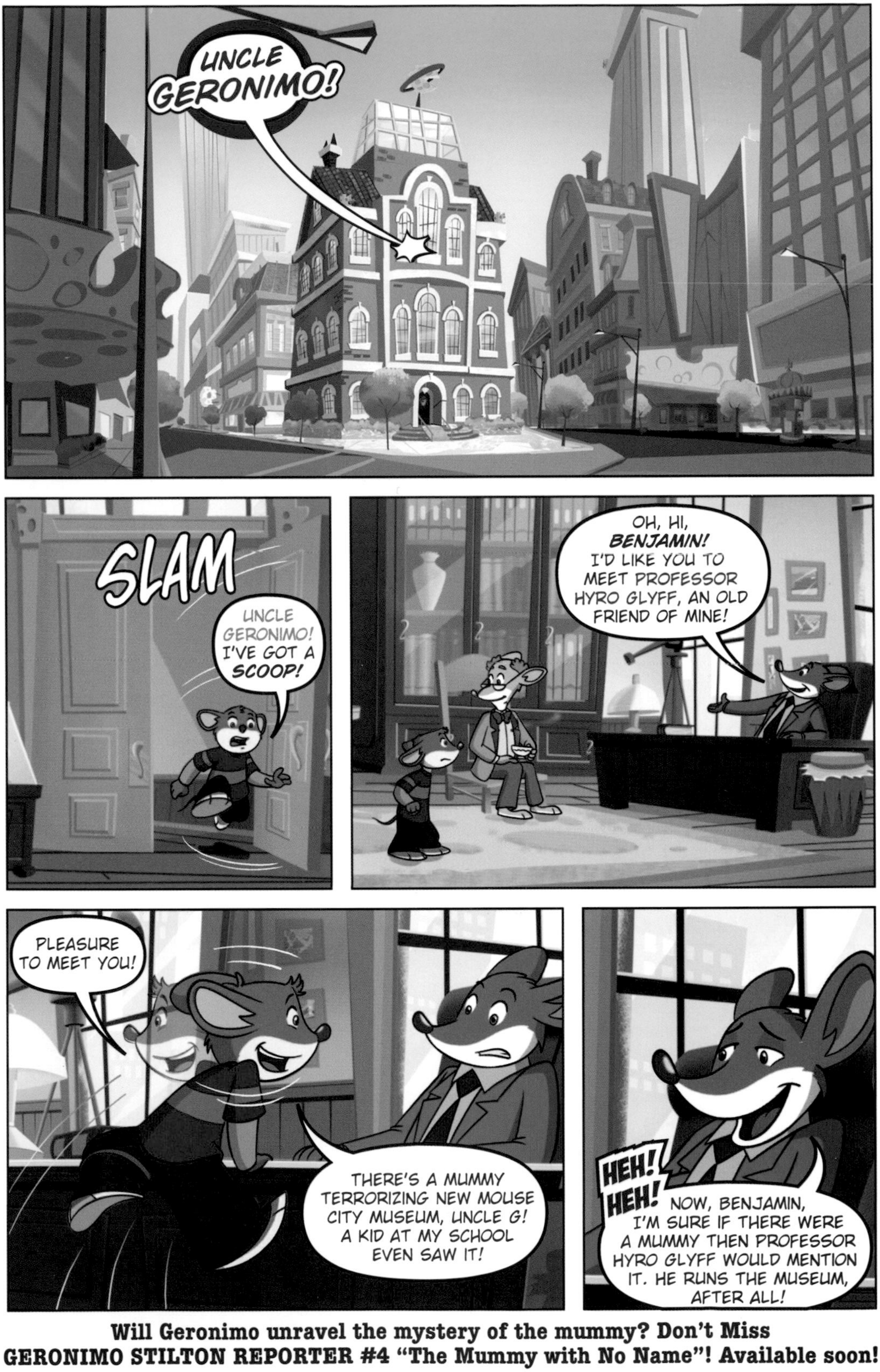
UNCLE GERONIMO!
SLAM
UNCLE GERONIMO! I'VE GOT A SCOOP!
OH, HI, BENJAMIN! I'D LIKE YOU TO MEET PROFESSOR HYRO GLYFF, AN OLD FRIEND OF MINE!
PLEASURE TO MEET YOU!
THERE'S A MUMMY TERRORIZING NEW MOUSE CITY MUSEUM, UNCLE G! A KID AT MY SCHOOL EVEN SAW IT!
HEH! HEH!
NOW, BENJAMIN, I'M SURE IF THERE WERE A MUMMY THEN PROFESSOR HYRO GLYFF WOULD MENTION IT. HE RUNS THE MUSEUM, AFTER ALL!

Will Geronimo unravel the mystery of the mummy? Don't Miss GERONIMO STILTON REPORTER #4 "The Mummy with No Name"! Available soon!

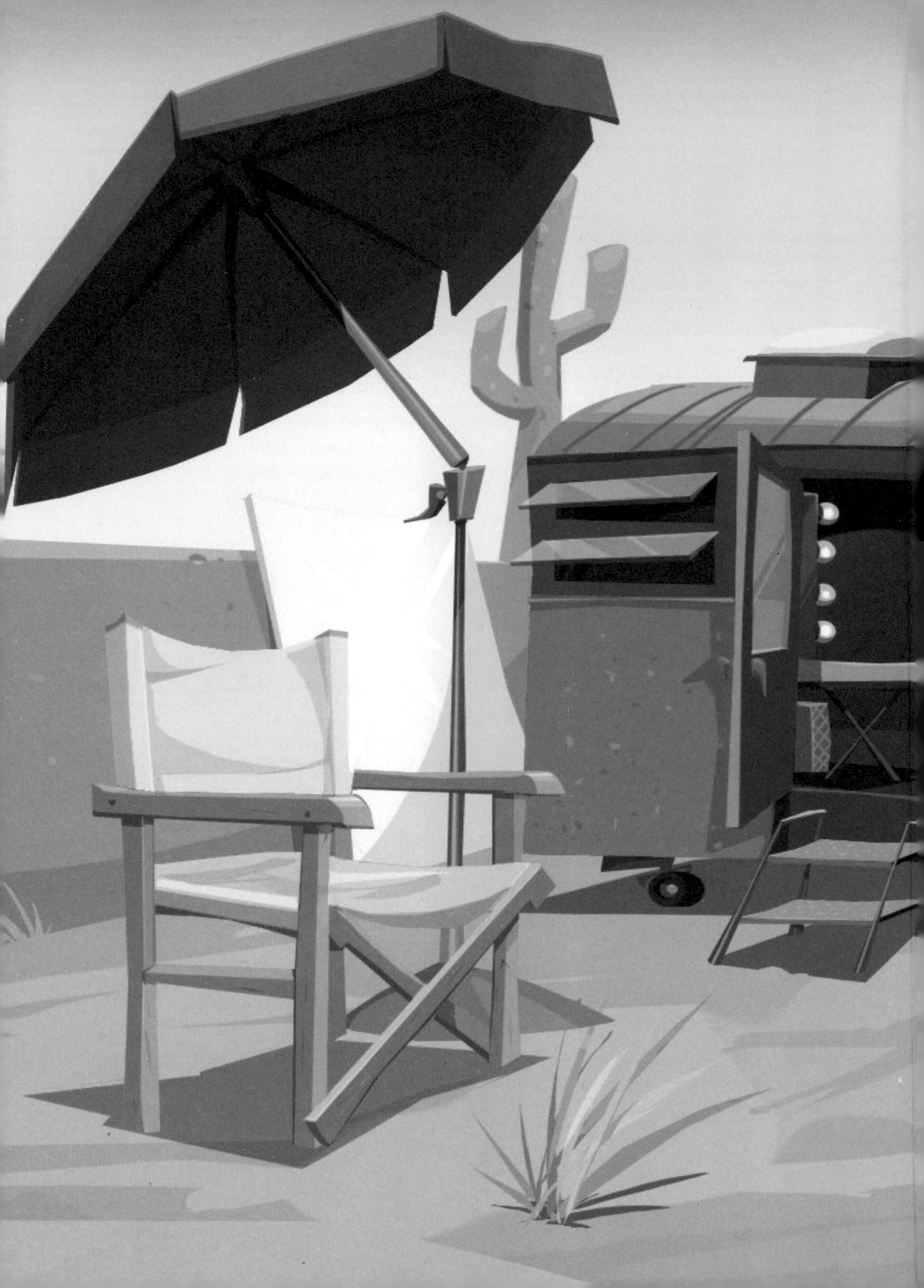